Vicious Circle

Vicious Circle

Helena Pielichaty

Oxford University Press

Oxford New York Toronto

Oxford University Press, Great Clarendon Street, Oxford OX2 6DP

Oxford New York
Athens Auckland Bangkok Bogota Bombay
Buenos Aires Calcutta Cape Town Dar es Salaam Delhi
Florence Hong Kong Istanbul Karachi
Kuala Lumpur Madras Madrid Melbourne
Mexico City Nairobi Paris Singapore
Taipei Tokyo Toronto Warsaw

and associated companies in
Berlin Ibadan

Oxford is a trade mark of Oxford University Press

A CIP catalogue record for this book is available
from the British Library

Cover illustration by Daniel Norman

ISBN 0 19 271775 8

Printed and bound in Great Britain by
Biddles Ltd, Guildford and King's Lynn

For Peter, Hanya, and Joe,
who gave me the space in which to write

And for Gwen Grant
who taught me how to write in the space

Vicious Circle

*'Why haven't we got any money? We've never got any money.
Why can't we be like other people and have fish and chips when
we fancy?'*

Ten-year-old Louisa May and her mother Georgette are
two of the 'have-nots', shuttling between ever-seedier
bed and breakfast accommodation. To help cope with
this way of life they play elaborate fantasy games,
pretending to be the characters in the romantic fiction
that Georgette borrows from the library in every town
they move to.

When they arrive at the Cliff Top Villas Hotel in a
run-down seaside resort and Georgette falls ill, it looks
as if the fantasy will have to end. But Louisa May enlists
the help of Joanna, another hotel resident, and together
they determine to find out the truth behind Georgette's
'let's pretend' existence. Maybe this way there will be a
chance for them to break out of the vicious circle and
become 'haves' at last . . .

HELENA PIELICHATY was born in Sweden to an English
mother and Polish-Russian father. Her family moved to
Yorkshire when Helena was five where she lived until
qualifying as a teacher from Bretton Hall College in
1978. She has taught in various parts of the country
including East Grinstead, Oxford, and Sheffield. Helena
now lives with her husband, who is also half-Polish, in
Nottinghamshire where she divides her time between
looking after their two children, writing, teaching, and
following the trials and tribulations of Huddersfield
Town A.F.C.

One

'This is it, Louisa May.'

Louisa May nodded. 'I thought it might be.'

'Cliff Top Villas Hotel. Isn't it splendid? Just as we'd imagined.'

'Better. Look at the pretty garden full of flowers and all the rooms have their own balcony. We'll be able to sit outside and watch the sun set over the sea.'

'We're going to have a lovely holiday here, I just know it.'

'I hope so, Mama, we deserve a treat.'

'You are so right.'

Georgette swooped to kiss the top of her daughter's head. 'There's probably a butler called Perkins and a chambermaid called Sally-Anne waiting inside. They'll be drinking China tea and eating homemade seed cake while they muse about us, their important guests.'

Louisa May sighed. She was tired now and her tight shoes had rubbed blisters on her heels after the walk up the steep hill. She struggled to release her two carrier bags which had entwined themselves into her fingers like plastic creepers. Cliff Top Villas Hotel was a dump.

There was no front garden, only a concreted forecourt enclosed by a low breeze-block wall. Discarded polystyrene food-trays, streaked with curry stains, gathered forlornly in damp corners. Louisa May quickly surveyed the front of the hotel, with its paint-starved woodwork and filthy bay windows, its lopsided 'vacancies' sign thrust against drab, grey, net curtains. She knew the best they could hope for was a lavatory that flushed.

Georgette peered uncertainly at the row of buttons which sprouted from the inside of the doorway, fumbling to release her own carrier bags and therefore the rest of all they owned, so she could ring the bell.

Louisa May turned from the house and gazed across the road. For the first time that day, her spirits rose. On the long walk up Cliff Bank, head down against the wind, eyes fixed on Georgette's purple boots, she hadn't seen the houses give way to clumps of sand-clogged grass that marked a boundary between road and cliff-edge. Nor had she been aware of the choppy sea sparkling in the bay beneath. It looked wonderful.

She hadn't wanted to move this time. She'd liked living in Lincoln, even if it had only been in a squat behind the crisp factory. She'd liked the swans on the river and the cold peace that filled her inside the cathedral. And the Social had promised a place of their own, in time. But then the letters had arrived, and for once Georgette had been quick and decisive. They had to leave. Again.

Louisa May had cried and made her mother choose somewhere nice, like the seaside. So here they were, somewhere along the east coast, in an unknown resort called Wathsea. Waiting.

'Yeah?'

The voice was deep and gruff. Louisa May spun round immediately and stood at her mother's side, where she knew she'd be needed.

Georgette cleared her throat. 'Good afternoon, Mr Putlock, I'm Mrs Van Der Lees and this is my daughter, Louisa May. I believe you are expecting us? My agent made a reservation on our behalf earlier today for a double room with all facilities.'

She smiled politely at the man staring rudely at her,

appearing not to notice he was only wearing a bath towel tied loosely round his flabby middle and that water dripped in dark streams down his hairy legs.

'I was in the bath,' he grumbled.

'If you could kindly show us to our room, we are both in urgent need of refreshing ourselves before we dine,' Louisa May's mother continued.

The man scratched at the flesh beneath the towel. 'What are you on about?'

Louisa May sighed. Georgette had forgotten to go back to normal again. Forgotten that people didn't play pretend like they did. She'd have to do the talking. She hated having to do the talking.

'Erm . . . Mrs Chambers sent us . . . she said she'd telephoned to check it was all right . . . that you did rooms for people like us.'

A look of dislike flicked over the man's face. 'Chambers? That mardy piece from the Social, you mean?' Louisa May nodded, as if agreeing with him, although she'd liked Mrs Chambers. Mrs Chambers had been kind, speaking patiently to Georgette and giving them tea and chocolate marshmallows. They didn't usually do that. Perhaps everyone was kinder at the seaside.

'Young man, our room, please.' Georgette arched her left eyebrow expressively. Her feet were beginning to ache too.

'Now just hang on a minute you, with your young man and rooms with all facilities. I've told them down there before: no kids, no druggies, and no weirdos. You're all three by the looks of it.'

'Quite. Standards are so important. Now is there a porter to attend to our luggage?'

'Mum,' Louisa May pleaded in a small voice.

'Yes, dear?'

'Let's not play the game until we get inside.'

'Try not to interrupt while I'm dealing with the proprietor, darling. We mustn't appear to be rude, must we?'

The half-naked proprietor snorted. 'Hey, Wanda,' he shouted over his shoulder into the dark hallway. He waited a few seconds. 'Wanda! Come and sort this lot out.'

There was a stone in Louisa May's left shoe. She could feel it jabbing through her sock. She couldn't wait for tomorrow. Tomorrow she could have some new shoes. New shoes that didn't squash her feet and make her toes burn like the ones she was wearing. New shoes from a proper shoe shop.

The door opened further. A woman with yolk-yellow hair piled high on top of her head emerged. The hair was pulled back so tightly it seemed to stretch her face along with it, making it seem pinched and plucked.

'What's up now? You know I'm doing me nails for tonight.' She held her freshly painted talons in front of her face, pleased with the results.

'Sort these two out before I freeze to death. They're from the Social.'

Once again, Louisa May felt the sting of cold eyes judging her.

'You're not New Age, are you? We don't want none of them, with their mucky dogs and mucky habits.'

'I've already told them that. She's not right, that one. Another loony to add to the pack. We'll have a full set soon if we don't watch it.' The man scowled at Georgette before disappearing inside.

Wanda scratched her shoulder. She looked searchingly at Georgette, who was fanning her face against an imagined heat. In their game, it was the height of summer, not the end of October.

Louisa May shuffled awkwardly. She knew her mother appeared odd, in her baggy jumpers and thin skirts layered over and over each other like bun cases, but the more you wore, the less you carried. It made things easier when travelling. She wished Georgette hadn't draped that mangy fox-fur round her neck, though, or stuck glass beads and hat pins at all angles through her black hat. It made her look like a little girl playing at dressing-up.

Wanda was staring at Louisa May now; staring at her spindly legs and charity shop clothes, at her gritty uncut hair and pale thin face. 'Have you got your giro?' she demanded.

'Yes. Mrs Chambers gave it to us.'

Wanda shrugged. 'You can come in then, but remember it's only temp'ry. Come April, you're out. We only take in your lot from the Social to tide us through the winter. Nobody comes to Wathsea in winter. There's nothing to come for.' She paused, as if waiting to be contradicted, but they had already passed through the town, with its desolate sea-front and dilapidated hotels. The only surprise was that people came at all.

'Do you think it would be possible to show us to our room now? We do seem to have been waiting a dreadfully long time.' It was Georgette in her 'dealing-with-the-servants' voice. Louisa May grimaced. She lifted her eyes cautiously to see how the landlady would react.

Wanda's dark eyebrows narrowed. 'Oh, I do beg your pardon, your ladyship, whatever can I 'ave been thinking of? Do come in and allow me to escort you to your room. And I do apologize for the lacking of the red carpet but one of the queen's corgis did a poopy on it on their last visit and it's not beck from the dry cleaners yet.'

Louisa May's face burned as she followed her mother indoors. Come April you're out, Eggy-hair had said. If they lasted a week it would be a miracle.

Two

Their room was at the far end of the dingy second-floor landing. A familiar smell of damp and dogs clung to the stale air. To Louisa May, houses like this always smelt of dogs, even when there weren't any.

'Right, here we are then, the Royal Suite,' Wanda continued in her fake posh voice. She opened the door ceremoniously, allowing Georgette to lead the way.

They had lived in worse places. At least the wallpaper wasn't peeling off and there was glass in the windows, unlike their basement room in Lincoln. Their two divan beds were draped in lurid orange coverlets, separated by a cheap, laminated dressing table. The curtains were too short for the window, the carpet too long for the room. It curled up at each end like stale toast.

Wanda began to fire instructions at them. 'The toilet's at the end of the landing. Provide your own paper. No cooking in your room but there is coffee and tea making facilities. You'll need fifty pences for the electric. Breakfast's between seven and eight-thirty sharp. Ambrose and me don't cash cheques or lend money or stand for late payments. If you was proper guests it'd be different but me and Ambrose have found it best to let people like you keep yourselves to yourselves.' Wanda spoke directly to Louisa May, who nodded.

'And bathing arrangements?' Georgette enquired, as she slowly plucked off her evening gloves, a finger at a time.

'Bathing arrangements?' asked Wanda, watching the much-practised routine with curiosity.

'I notice our room is not en-suite.'

'You'll also notice it's not the 'ilton, neither. You've got a sink and there's a bath next to the toilet. Beggars can't be choosers, you know!'

Louisa May stiffened. They might be homeless but they had never begged yet. Georgette carefully laid down her gloves on the bed.

'Very well. That will be all, Mrs Putlock.'

'Not quite all, Mrs . . . ?'

'Mrs Van Der Lees.'

'Mrs Vandaleese? Very posh. Foreign, is it?'

'Dutch.'

'Thought so. We get a lot of foreigners staying here. Stands to reason. No state handouts where they come from, is there?'

'Was there anything else?' Georgette asked.

'Just your giro to sort out.'

'Giro?' Georgette sounded as though it was something she'd never heard of in her life instead of something that had helped her through the past nine years. Wanda watched Georgette's reaction closely. Something in her eyes flickered then changed.

'The . . . er . . . docket Mrs Chambers gave you down at the Social. I can deal with it for you; it'd be no bother. Save you all that inconvenience of having to queue up with those rough types you get down there. A lady like you doesn't want to have to do that.' Wanda's voice was silky-smooth without a trace of the earlier mockery.

'It would save me a lot of time and allow my daughter and I the chance to become acclimatized to our surroundings,' Georgette agreed.

'Dead right. You get your feet up—rest them pretty ankles.'

8

Georgette unclipped her sequined evening bag and began to sort carefully through its contents.

'Now, let me see where I placed it.'

'I like to help whenever I can,' Wanda said. She was almost pleasant now, smiling down at Louisa May. Louisa May didn't smile back. She knew her game.

Wanda's eyes brightened as Georgette withdrew a brown envelope from her bag.

'Just sign it at the back, love. That gives me permission to cash it, as your agent. I do it for most of the residents.'

'Certainly, and as you have been so helpful I wish you to take a shilling from the change, to compensate you for your trouble.' Georgette signed the cheque with a flourish and handed it over to Wanda. Wanda glanced briefly at the amount shown on the cheque and her mouth puckered greedily. Anger surged through Louisa May like a stab of hunger. She knew there was extra money on the cheque, a clothing allowance for when she started at her new school. Georgette was going to hand over all the money they had to this horrible witch with yellow hair. They'd never see any of it.

'Mum,' Louisa May's voice faltered.

'Not now, dear.'

'Mum.'

'Not now, dear. It's rude to interrupt.'

'But, Mum, Mrs Chambers said to cash it yourself. She told you twice.'

Wanda interrupted swiftly. 'Oh, her. Doesn't know a thing, if you ask me.'

'Well, nobody is asking you, are they?' Louisa May burst out.

'Louisa May! How dare you be so disrespectful! Apologize at once to Mrs Putlock!' Two bright pink spots flared against Georgette's hollow cheeks as she stared in dismay at her daughter.

Louisa May glared stubbornly at the bitty, turquoise carpet. Wanda sniffed. 'Kids, eh? They've got that much lip. I'm glad me and Ambrose never had any.' She carefully folded the brown envelope and slipped it into her pocket.

'If you could leave us now, Mrs Putlock,' Georgette asked politely.

'Right you are. I'll go cash this for you. It should just about cover two weeks board and lodgings.' The landlady closed the door behind her, leaving a faint odour of cigarettes and sweat. Louisa May threw herself down on to the nearest bed and sank her face into the orange cover. It smelt of cat pee.

'Louisa May, whatever have I done to deserve this behaviour?' Georgette asked in a concerned voice.

'Beggars can't be choosers,' Louisa May answered, curling herself into a tight ball.

Three

Louisa May must have fallen asleep because when she awoke the room was darker. Her mother was sitting upright against the headrest of her bed, reading. She had already unpacked her own things. The three carrier bags were folded in neat squares on the dressing table.

Steam arose from the sink, misting the cracked blue tiles above it. That would be their underwear soaking. Washing their pants and socks was always the first thing Georgette did when they arrived in a new place. They didn't have enough knickers to allow them to stockpile and sometimes they had to share.

'Is there anything to eat?' Louisa May asked. Georgette didn't hear her. Once she started reading, she entered another world. Her books were stacked beside her bed in three knee-high columns. Each pile a carrier bag full.

'Mum!' Louisa May repeated. 'Mum!'

'Mmm?' Georgette asked, turning a page.

'I'm hungry.'

'Get something to eat then.'

'What?'

'Whatever you want.'

'OK. I'll ring Perkins and ask him to bring me a pizza, shall I?' Georgette dragged her eyes away from her book, smiling as Louisa May, pretending her hand was a telephone, spoke poshly into the 'receiver'. 'Hello, room service? I'd like a very, very large pizza, please, with tons of cheese. And fifteen bottles of Coca Cola. No, not Diet Coke, real Coke. Room five, please. That's right, the

Van Der Lees apartment, at the double. Thank you.' She 'hung up'. 'Van Der Lees! Where did you dig that one up from?' Georgette tapped the cover of the book she was reading. Louisa May bent forward to see what it said. *The Temptations of Rosanna Van Der Lees.* She groaned. 'Not her again.'

'She's great. I've almost read the whole series. This is the last one.'

Louisa May raised her eyes to the ceiling. 'Thank you, God.'

Georgette began to quote from the book. ' "Rosanna sighed as the scent of honeysuckle drifted towards her from the garden below. If only Gilbert were here to share her bliss." ' Georgette paused dreamily. 'Isn't that wonderful? Can't you just smell that honeysuckle?'

'I can't smell anything except your feet. It's daft, like all the stuff you read. Daft and soppy.'

'It's daft! It's daft!' Georgette threw the book down and leapt off the bed. She lunged at Louisa May who screeched as she tried to dodge Georgette's dangerous fingers.

'Don't! Don't!' Louisa May shrieked with excitement, trying to struggle free. This was more like it. Her mother, dressed in her old leggings and tatty jumper, playing and being silly. After a while, Georgette sat back on her bed, breathless from their play-acting. Louisa May tried again with the food.

'Really though, can't we go downstairs and see what time dinner's ready?' she pleaded.

The light died in her mother's eyes. Georgette fastened a strand of lank hair behind her ear and sighed heavily, as if all her energy had been squeezed out of her in one long breath. 'You go, I'll rinse out the smalls and finish unpacking.'

'I don't want to go on my own.'

'You'll be all right.' Georgette crossed over to the sink and began half-heartedly pumping the wet clothes around, her thin shoulder blades as sharp as shark fins through her worn jumper. 'I'm not hungry.'

Louisa May traced a circle on the bedcover with her finger, running round and round it with her nail.

'Why did you give that woman all our money?' she asked quietly.

Georgette stopped washing for a second.

'She'll bring it back.'

'How do you know?' Louisa May persisted. Her mother was usually so careful with their money; it had been a shock to see her hand over the giro so readily. Georgette squeezed out a pair of socks and set them down against the splashback, turned and smiled.

'She'll bring it back, I promise.'

Louisa May's stomach growled painfully before she could answer.

'You'd better find that pizza,' Georgette ordered.

Outside the room, the landing was dark and narrow. Louisa May hurried down the stairs then stopped at the bottom. There were a number of doors leading off from the draughty hallway. The one furthest away was closed, with 'Private' written at the top. Next to it were two more doors, both slightly ajar. One of these would be the dining room, the other the lounge. That was the usual set-up in these places. She hoped the evening meal was the sort where you helped yourself. If so, she'd just grab whatever there was and take it back upstairs.

Louisa May sniffed. She could smell fried fish. Fish and chips were her favourite. Happily, she pushed open the door and wondered whether there'd be seconds. But it wasn't the dining room she entered, only the lounge.

13

There were fish and chips but they were being eaten out of a crater of grease-soaked newspaper by a woman sitting in an armchair. She looked up guiltily when Louisa May entered and paused with a chip half-way to her mouth.

'Oh,' she said and ate the chip hurriedly. Louisa May stood in the doorway, not sure what to do. The woman smiled and pointed to her fish and chips. 'Will you help me finish these? I'll never get rid of them before they go cold.'

Louisa May shook her head. Hungry as she was, she knew not to take food from strangers. 'I'm waiting for the evening meal,' she said.

The woman took a swig from a can of Coke at her feet.

'Huh! I wouldn't bother if I were you.'

'Why?'

'Well, A, you'll have to wait until seven o'clock and B, the food is revolting.'

Louisa May's stomach growled loudly. 'I can't wait until then. It's only five o'clock now!'

'Have some chips, then. You can see I shouldn't be eating all these calories,' the woman offered, patting her rounded stomach. Louisa May didn't move. Keen eyes probed hers. 'You do right to refuse, though I promise I'm harmless. Where's your mum and dad?'

'My mum's upstairs.'

'Oh.' The woman set down the fish and chips on the chair beside her. Louisa May reckoned she looked like a coconut. She was definitely as oval as one but it was the hair that did it; although it was short at the sides, a stubborn, ginger tuft sprouted proudly skywards from the crown just like a coconut's. The coconut grinned.

'Welcome to Putlock's Palace. I'm Joanna Frankish, room four.'

'That's the room next to us. I'm Louisa May.'

'Louisa May? Not plain old Louisa?'

'No. Louisa May. After Louisa May Alcott, who wrote *Little Women*.'

'Very posh. A bit long, though. Can I call you Lou instead?'

Louisa May shook her head again. 'My mum thinks it's vulgar to shorten names.'

'Oh, that's a shame. I think Lou's more . . . cute American kid.'

Louisa May beamed. She liked the idea. 'Well, gee thanks, ma'am.'

Joanna laughed, a crackling laugh that made her chin wobble. 'What if I just call you Lou when we're by ourselves? So, have you got any brothers or sisters, Lou? Any Enids or Roalds?'

'No, there's just me and my mum. She's called Georgette.'

'Don't tell me. After Georgette Heyer, writer of historical romantic fiction, right?'

'Right.'

'My nan's got all hers. Hey, your dad's not called Charles Dickens by any chance?'

'No, Daniel Brody,' Louisa May smiled. Joanna seemed friendly and she had a nice way of talking, like the pretty lady on *Blue Peter*. Perhaps she could be trusted with The Story.

'The nurse who found my mum was reading a book by Georgette Heyer and that's why they named her Georgette.'

'Found her?'

Louisa May nodded and sidled further into the room

but still keeping a distance between them. She loved telling this. 'Yes. When she was a new-born baby my mum was left in a hospital dustbin and nearly died.' It had actually been a corridor outside the baby-care unit but Louisa May thought a dustbin was more dramatic.

'A dustbin? I know cuts in the health service are bad but that's taking things a bit too far. Did anyone find out who left her there?'

Louisa May continued solemnly. 'No. My mum was brought up in a children's home and nobody there knew anything. But last year a woman called Wendy Almond started writing to us, which is strange because we never get letters. My mum says that must be her mum trying to find her because that's what women do when they've let their babies be adopted. They wait until you're all grown up then come looking for you to say sorry but Wendy Almond can get lost because we're not interested. In fact, mum says she doesn't want to see her until she's on her death bed and then only to spit in her eye!'

Joanna looked surprised at the girl's anger but replied evenly, 'Good for her. Still, I suppose this Wendy Almond must have had her reasons.'

'Mum says there can't be any reasons for abandoning your own child. She hates even talking about it. They tried to take me into care once but she wouldn't let them.'

Joanna drained her can. She looked with renewed interest at the young girl in front of her. 'Why don't you sit down. Tell me all about yourself? I bet you've had a fascinating life.'

Louisa May bit her lip. She'd gone too far already. 'We're just normal, like everyone else.'

'Of course you are, everyone I know was born in a dustbin!'

'Not born in a dustbin, found in a dustbin,' Louisa May corrected.

'Sorry, found in a dustbin.'

'We're just normal.'

'So you said. Are you sure you won't sit down? It's not much but it's home!' Joanna joked. Louisa May looked around. It was a dingy room with a huge wooden sideboard pushed against the chimney breast. Around this huddled five dilapidated armchairs facing a dust-covered television set.

Joanna's eyes followed hers. 'No use looking at that thing, it's broken. One of the previous residents thought he was a surgeon and took all its insides out. It's a laugh a minute in this place, girl.'

Louisa May's heart sank. She liked television. Joanna stood up and pushed the fish paper down the side of the chair.

'How long have you been here?' Louisa May asked.

'Since the end of June when I left university with a Geography degree but without a job. I worked in a rock factory during the summer but it was only seasonal and I've just stayed on. This place kind of suits my mood.'

Louisa May gazed longingly at the broken television, not really listening. 'What do you do at night if there's no telly?' she asked, more to herself than Joanna.

Joanna hesitated. 'I have a TV in my room. You can watch that whenever you want to. It'll be nice to have company other than woodlice and spiders. I warn you, though, I'm allergic to anything Australian.'

'Honest? I can watch whenever I want? That's cool. I'll have to ask my mum first.'

The television owner rummaged around in her shoulder bag. 'Here, cop this.' She threw an apple towards Louisa May who caught it against her chest.

'And these.' A packet of peanuts was lobbed in the same direction. 'Emergency rations, for those at peril on the sea or kids named after famous writers.'

'Thanks, Coconut.' The nickname slipped out without thinking. Joanna patted her spiky hair and giggled.

'Well, I've been called worse!'

Louisa May returned happily to her room, glad to have met someone nice at the hotel.

Four

When Louisa May bounced into their room, she found her mother crying. Large, bulbous tears ran freely down her cheeks.

'What's wrong, Mum?'

'He's dead, Louisa May, he's dead.'

'Who?'

'Gilbert.'

'Gilbert?'

'Gilbert Farthingale, Rosanna's fiancé. He's been killed in a duel.'

'Oh, is that all?'

'It's so cruel. Her first fiancé died of cholera, her second died saving a child from drowning, and now poor Gilbert.'

'She should choose them better.'

'It's so, so sad.'

'Someone gave me an apple and some peanuts.'

Georgette looked up immediately.

'Who?' she asked sharply.

'A woman called Joanna Frankish. She looks like a coconut and eats a lot.'

'Oh, well, wash it first.' Louisa May rinsed the apple, noting their underwear was still in the sink.

'There's no food until seven o'clock so can we go and get some fish and chips?'

'We've no money until tomorrow.'

Louisa May tutted. It was always the same.

'Why haven't we got any money? We've never got any money. Why can't we be like other people and have fish and chips when we fancy?'

Her mother continued to read but replied calmly. 'We're not other people, Louisa May, and we've been over this a thousand times. To have money you have to have a job. To have a job you need somewhere to live. If you want to live somewhere you have to have money. I haven't got a job so we haven't got any money. Because we have no money we haven't got a house. We are the "have-nots" of this world.'

Louisa May nodded at this well-worn phrase. 'It'd be different if Dad was here, wouldn't it? We'd have a proper house then, wouldn't we?'

Georgette frowned, bending the spine of her book back irritably. 'If you say so.'

Louisa May knew these conversations never got her anywhere but she persisted in them anyway. 'He's been at sea since before I was born. He must be due a break by now. Even Captain Bligh came home in the end.' Sea adventures were the only stories she ever read willingly. Her observation fell on deaf ears. 'Tell me about him,' she pleaded.

'You know all there is to know,' Georgette muttered.

'Tell me anyway.'

'Your father's name was Daniel Brody. He was brought up in the same home as I was but we never spoke to each other until we were sixteen . . . '

'Because you were both too shy.'

'Then, a week before I was supposed to leave the home . . . '

'Because you were nearly seventeen and too old to stay.'

'He left a red rose on top of a book I was reading . . . '

' . . . *Rebecca* by Daphne Du Maurier.'

Georgette scowled. 'Who's telling the story here?' Louisa May sat upright and pulled a pretend zip across her mouth, allowing her mother to continue. 'Then, the night before I had to leave he knocked quietly on my bedroom door and when I answered he kissed me softly on the lips and said, "I will always love you." The next day I learned he had run away to sea, never to return. That kiss changed my life. A little while later I found out I was going to have a baby.'

'Me,' interrupted Louisa May.

'And because of this miracle I was allowed to stay on at the home until you were born.'

'Then they tried to take me away from you so you could finish your studies because you were brainy. I'm glad you didn't let them,' said Louisa May hotly.

Georgette stroked Louisa May's hair. 'Nobody will ever take you away, Louisa May. That's a promise.'

'I wish Wendy Almond hadn't left you.'

Georgette breathed in sharply. 'Why do you keep bringing her up?'

'Sorry.'

'The only time I want to see that woman is when?'

'When you're on your death bed so you can spit in her eye,' Louisa May chanted loyally. 'I know. I'm sorry.'

Georgette returned to her novel while Louisa May took a thoughtful bite from her apple. She was about to swallow when the whole room shook. Windows rattled and several books slid on to the carpet. Within seconds their door handle twisted and Mrs Wanda Putlock stormed into their room, thrusting a brown envelope at Georgette.

'Right you, Mrs Vanderleese from 'olland, I'm giving you one first and final warning. If you ever, ever, muck me around again you and that kid of yours are straight out on the street with all the other rubbish. Have you got that?'

Georgette hunched back on her bed and continued to read.

'I'm talking to you, lady!' Wanda screeched.

Georgette slowly looked up from her book. 'Does there seem to be a problem, Mrs Putlock?' she asked coolly.

Wanda almost growled her reply. 'Don't you Mrs Putlock me. I've never been so showed up in all my life when I tried to cash this with your false signature on it. Vanderleese, my foot. You're a Haddock!'

'By name if not by nature,' Georgette drawled.

'Don't you be clever with me, I'm warning you. Live in my house, live by my rules. Now I want my rent by lunchtime tomorrow or you are out of here. Is that clear?'

Georgette seemed immune to Wanda's anger. She yawned widely and picked up her book.

'And what's more,' Wanda continued, 'as you haven't paid for anything yet, you are not entitled to an evening meal, nor breakfast, so don't bother coming down for none until I see some money up front.'

'Your hospitality is overwhelming us, madam. Rarely have we received such a cordial welcome. Do close the door after you on the way out, there's a good servant.'

Wanda's eyes narrowed uncertainly. Georgette seemed to be serious. She was obviously unhinged. The landlady turned instead to Louisa May. 'I'd make that last if I were you,' she warned, staring at the uneaten apple in her hand. She tossed the envelope on to Louisa May's lap, then flounced out, leaving the door wide open.

Louisa May finally chewed the pulpy apple in her mouth. It was warm and tasteless and nearly impossible to swallow.

'I told you we'd get our money back,' Georgette stated, returning to Gilbert's funeral.

Five

Louisa May waited impatiently outside the lavatory, hopping from one foot to the other, praying whoever was in there would be quick. From downstairs, the smell of bacon and the clatter of cutlery told her it was breakfast time but she wasn't bothered. In an hour she'd have her shoes and after that, a burger. Her mother had promised.

The lavatory door creaked open and Louisa May stood aside. An old woman with straggly, gypsum-coloured hair emerged looking worried and flustered. She peered at Louisa May in the dim light. 'Where's Emerald?' she asked.

'I don't know.' Louisa May saw that the woman's cardigan was buttoned up all wrong, and she had her blouse on inside-out, its label jutting from under her chin, like she sometimes did when she'd been getting changed in a hurry after school games.

'Where's Emerald?' the woman asked again, staring with watery eyes.

'I don't know.' Louisa May slid past and bolted the door.

'Where's Emerald?' the voice pursued from the corridor.

Louisa May paused to listen before carefully wiping the cracked seat and sitting down. She'd met old people like this before. They rooted about in litter bins or shouted swear words at statues. It was best to ignore them. They couldn't help it.

Back in her room, Louisa May watched her mother getting ready. Today Georgette was dressed in black apart from her purple boots and the fox-fur. As a finishing touch, she had pinned black netting around the rim of her bonnet, so that it descended unevenly to her chin like a bee-keeper's hat. 'Why are you wearing that?' Louisa May asked in disgust.

'Out of respect for Gilbert Farthingale.'

'But he's not real.'

'He was real to me, and as such, I feel it only right that I mourn his passing.'

'People will stare.'

'People will stare anyway. They always do.'

That was true enough. Louisa May shrugged and fastened her jacket. What did it matter as long as she got her shoes?

Batty's Footwear shop towered between an empty ice-cream parlour and a wig-maker's establishment. They were the only three shops in Wathsea which had kept their Edwardian façades. Ornately-patterned tiles surrounded Batty's two display windows which curved inwards to meet a pair of heavy mahogany doors. As it was Saturday morning, these had been pushed open to entice customers inside.

'Those are the ones I like.' Louisa May pointed out the shoes. They were part of a neat display of children's footwear arranged against a backdrop of plastic green grass and paper leaves. 'Give Autumn a Kickstart with Kickstart Kids Shoes,' the poster urged.

'Hmm,' said Georgette, lifting her veil slightly to see the shoes more clearly.

'They're nice, aren't they?' Louisa May asked, admiring the bright patent leather and jazzy multi-coloured laces.

'Hmm.'

'And we have got the money.' She knew they had. They had waited ten minutes for the post office to open and a further five minutes for Georgette to sort out indentification to prove she was who the giro said she was.

'We've got some money,' Georgette corrected, 'some money, most of which we owe to Cliff Top Villas.' Louisa May swallowed hard. What if her mother broke her promise? She was so unpredictable. But she had to have those shoes.

'Mrs Chambers said . . . '

'Mrs Chambers doesn't live in the real world.' Louisa May stared at her mother, at her black stick of a body with her stupid hat and hideous fox-fur. Which real world did she have in mind?

Georgette opened her purse slightly and ran a satin-gloved fingertip over the tuft of banknotes. 'All right, darling. Kickstarts it is.'

Louisa May planted a dry kiss on the fox's nose. 'Yes!' she hissed at it. 'Thank you!'

The shop was already busy. Assistants flitted between customer and storeroom carrying piles of boxes to and fro. Above them, a digital counter flashed a new number when they were ready to serve the next customer. Louisa May timidly pulled their ticket from the machine. Twenty-six. The digital counter was on twenty-three.

She sat back on the rich velvet of her chair, twisting her number around her thumb. She'd never been in a shop like this before. They usually kept to the charity stalls on markets. Her present shoes had been given to her from a school's lost property box.

Across from where Louisa May was sitting, a mother was arguing with her two children, a boy and a girl.

'I want new shoes and new trainers, Mummy, I told you. And I have to have Ace-make trainers like Josh, or else,' the boy demanded.

'Well, if he's having new trainers I'm having some as well as my party ones!' his sister whined.

Their mother laughed. 'Oh, you poor, deprived things. Better do as they ask or we'll never hear the end of it.' She smiled at the shop assistant, who smiled back indulgently.

'Of course, madam.'

Louisa May watched as the assistant slid the measure on to the girl's foot. The girl was wearing thick pink socks that looked cosy and soft. Louisa May glanced down at her own feet and felt herself growing hot. Her shoes were bad enough; scuffed and misshapen and dirty. But her socks were worse. They were dishwater grey and baggy where the stitching had unravelled. They were threadbare. They smelt.

She shifted uncomfortably in her chair. The girl opposite pushed away the shoes in the assistant's hand. They were black and shiny with multicoloured laces. Louisa May's shoes.

'There's no way I'm wearing those, Mummy. They are so gross!'

'Twenty-six?'

An assistant sought out his next customer, a false smile painted on his bored face. 'Twenty-six?' he called again. Slowly Louisa May raised the ticket in her hand. Her mother was reading.

'How may I help you?' the assistant asked. He was wearing a crisp white shirt with a nameplate pinned across the breast pocket informing them he was called Stephen. He looked down at both Georgette and Louisa May and his expression changed. The false smile softened as he knelt down in front of Louisa May but his eyes darted repeatedly towards Georgette. 'Who's for new shoes, then?' he asked.

He had very green eyes, Louisa May noticed, and his fair hair was tied firmly back into a pony tail. Louisa May's throat felt dry. She turned from his green eyes to the beautiful shoes the girl opposite had regarded as 'gross' and which the assistant had shoved to one side. She glanced briefly at her own feet. 'I think we've made a mistake,' she whispered.

Stephen bent closer to hear her.

'Why's that then?' he whispered back.

'Don't know.' Louisa May did know she wouldn't be able to talk any more. If they didn't leave now the tears would come.

Stephen glanced at Georgette, who turned a page and continued to read. 'Perhaps your mother could persuade you to stay?' he asked hopefully.

The question remained unanswered as Louisa May tugged fiercely at Georgette's sleeve. 'Mum, Mum!'

'Mmm?'

'We're going!'

'Have you chosen already?' Georgette asked in surprise, looking round for Louisa May, who was already half-way through the door. The assistant gazed after Georgette keenly until she, too, had disappeared.

'Twenty-seven?' he asked, boredom returning to his features.

Shoppers turned to stare as the pinched-faced little girl brushed past them. They stared again as a thin woman, dressed like something out of an old film, scurried after her. 'Louisa May! Wait!'

But Louisa May hurried on, barging into pushchairs and bulging carrier bags. It was only when she reached the end of Wathsea High Street and had to wait for the traffic to stop, that Georgette caught up with her.

'What's the matter? Why didn't you choose any shoes?'

'As if you don't know.'

'I don't know, that's why I'm asking.' Georgette panted for breath as they weaved between stationary traffic.

'You didn't want me to have any, did you? That's why I didn't bother because I knew you'd blame me for spending all your money.'

'That's not true.'

'It is.'

'I wanted you to have new shoes.'

'No, you didn't. You never said a thing in the shop.'

'I was reading.'

'Nobody else's mother reads in shoe shops.'

'I don't see why you can't read in shoe shops. People read in dentist's and doctor's so why not shoe shops?'

'It's not the same.'

All she had wanted was to be normal, like she had told Joanna they were. But normal was your mother joking with the assistant, not reading. Normal was being able to have your feet measured without being ashamed of your socks. They were nowhere near normal and never would be. And it hurt so much.

'You do need new shoes, Louisa May.'

'Oh, give her a prize!'

Louisa May knew she was being unfair, knew it was not Georgette's fault they did not have enough money, but she continued anyway. 'That other girl was getting two new pairs in one go.'

'I know.'

'How do you know? You were reading.'

'I don't read with my ears.'

'She had pink socks.'

'They were babyish.'

'I liked them.'

'OK, I'll buy you some pink socks.'

'I don't want any.'

'Louisa May?'

'What?'

'I'm sorry.'

Louisa May felt she was the one who should be saying sorry but she was still hurting too much. She carried on walking quickly, past the shops and the tacky amusement arcades, with 'closed until new season' stuck across their windows. Georgette didn't try to keep up but Louisa May was aware that she was behind her, clumping along in her heavy boots.

Only when they reached the bottom of Cliff Bank did Louisa May slow down. She was too close to the hotel now, too near its gloomy corridors and damp rooms, so when Georgette gently slipped her arm through hers she allowed it to stay.

They trudged on for a short while, taking slow, short steps. Both knew that the further away from Wathsea they were, the less chance there was of buying the shoes. When they reached the point where houses gave way to the cliff edge, it was too late to turn back. They both stopped, their eyes drawn to the sea. Georgette was hot and breathless, even from such a slow walk. 'We could go down to the beach?' she offered.

'You've got to pay the rent.'

'It can wait.'

'What if Mrs Putlock throws us out?'

'She won't. We're easy money to her.'

The memory of Wanda's spiteful words still scared Louisa May. 'Pay it first, please.'

Georgette unclipped her bag and slid three ten pound notes from her purse. She carefully folded them into a tight square then handed them to Louisa May.

'Take this,' she said. Louisa May held on to the money while Georgette pulled the fox-fur from round her neck. Stretching open the fox's stiff mouth, she snatched the notes from Louisa May's hand and quickly fed them into the fox's throat.

'Good idea, Mum,' Louisa May said proudly. 'Burglars wouldn't think of looking there.'

'Or landladies.' Georgette looped the pelt back round her neck. They had reached Cliff Top Villas by now. Georgette pushed open the door, turning to Louisa May before the darkness engulfed her, her face pale and sad. 'Sorry about your shoes.'

'Sorry for being rude.'

'You didn't really like those pink socks, did you?'

Louisa May shook her head. 'No—wouldn't be seen dead in them.'

Her mother stuck her nose in the air, imitating the little boy in the shop. 'I'm a spoilt brat and I must have forty pairs of shoes like Josh or else!'

They smiled knowingly at each other, as if sharing a secret. As Louisa May followed Georgette into the hotel, she tried not to think of her toes chafing in her old shoes. Instead, she fixed her attention on the fox's head which flopped lazily against her mother's shoulder and wondered what other secret treasures were trapped in its gullet along with the three ten pound notes.

Six

Louisa May waited outside the room while Georgette paid their rent. When she finally arrived Louisa May playfully grabbed her arm, tugging it up and down. 'Can we go down to the sea now? Please, please, please!' A walk along the beach would make up for the awful morning. Louisa May waited for the door to be unlocked before continuing hopefully. 'Go on! You said we could.'

But Georgette's eyes had that glazed-over look she hated. 'What did She say when you paid the rent?' Louisa May asked, guessing the change in mood must have something to do with their landlady.

Georgette stood upright in the centre of the room and took off her hat. Slowly, she began to unpick the black netting veil which drooped tiredly from the brim. At last she spoke. 'Dear Mrs Putlock accepted the payment with her usual degree of cordiality and good breeding.'

Louisa May's heart lurched. It was the Rosanna voice. She tried once more. 'Let's go to the beach. Come on. We've never been this near before.'

Her mother began to fill the kettle. 'I think some refreshment is in order.'

'After, then?' Louisa May pleaded.

Georgette glanced at a thick book lying unopened on her bed. Louisa May grimaced. 'Not reading. Not boring, boring reading.'

Her mother plugged the kettle into the socket then selected a sachet of coffee from the margarine tub on the dressing table. Her movements were slow and clumsy, as if even making a cup of coffee was too much effort.

She looked at her daughter wearily, her normal voice returning. 'I'm worn out, Louisa May. Maybe tomorrow, eh? It might be warmer tomorrow.'

Realizing her mother did look tired, Louisa May shrugged then reluctantly flicked through some of the books at her feet. They all looked alike to her with pictures of soppy women on the front gazing up at soppy men. She flipped over a cover. 'County Library Services' was stamped across the ticket slip.

It was the same in all the books, except the names of the towns changed, depending on where they'd been living at the time. Georgette had taken books from libraries everywhere. 'Extended borrowing', she called it, but Louisa May knew it was stealing, even if her mother did always send a note to the librarian.

'Dear Madam,' she'd write in her huge looping style, 'I regret to inform you that we are "between parlours" once again and must leave the region at once. Time prevents me from returning my volume but it will be well looked after. Yours sincerely Mrs G. Haddock.' The libraries never replied, or, if they did, it was long after they'd disappeared.

'You'll have to write to Lincoln library soon,' Louisa May said.

'Mmm?'

'To let them know we're "between parlours".'

Before she could reply, Georgette began to cough uncontrollably, her eyes bulging and watering at the same time. She pointed furiously at the toilet roll on the dressing table. Louisa May hurriedly tore away strips of paper and handed them to Georgette, who, doubled at the waist, felt for them blindly with her free hand. After a while the coughing stopped and Georgette slumped on to her bed.

'Ugh! I thought your teeth were going to fly out then!' Louisa May exclaimed, trying to joke away the coughing. Georgette was often ill and she hoped this was not the beginning of another bout of something she had picked up.

Her mother smiled weakly. 'It's all this fresh seaside air. I'm not used to it.' Behind them, the kettle clicked.

'I'll make your coffee,' Louisa May offered. Carefully, she poured the boiling water over the sticky granules in the cup, then pierced the lid of the tiny milk carton with her nail. 'Mum?'

'Mmm?'

'I'm sorry again about the shoes.'

Georgette took the cup Louisa May handed to her with eyes half-closed. 'We'll get them on Monday. I won't wear the veil.'

'It wasn't that . . . ' Louisa May's sentence trailed away unconvincingly. The veil had been part of it; she couldn't lie.

Her hesitation was met with understanding. 'You are so much sweeter than those children in the shop, with or without new shoes.'

Louisa May grinned. 'And you're the best mum in the world, with or without a wonky veil.'

'Well, I'm glad that's sorted. Now can I have my rest?'

'Sure, but I don't feel like reading. Can I do something else?'

'What like?'

'You know that Joanna I was telling you about, the one who gave me the apple and peanuts?'

'Yes.'

'Can I go and see if I can watch her telly? She said I could, anytime.'

Georgette coughed again, short, thick coughs which reddened her face deeper and deeper each time. She nodded briefly. 'As long as it's not a bother to her.'

'Thanks, Mum, you're cool!'

Georgette reached for more toilet roll. She felt anything but 'cool'.

There was no reply when Louisa May knocked on the door to room four. Dejected, she was about to turn away when she recognized Joanna's voice further along the corridor. She was trying to persuade someone to do something in the same wheedling tones Louisa May had used with Georgette earlier. 'Come on,' she was saying, 'come on, it'll do you good. A bit of fresh air. A walk on the beach. Oh, don't shake your head, Mrs Bannister. I know you'll enjoy yourself once you're out. You can't stay indoors all the time or you'll have bed sores as big as watermelons.'

As she came down the corridor towards her, Louisa May realized Joanna was with the old woman from that morning. This Mrs Bannister didn't want to be escorted, she was pulling back all the time and shaking her head. Joanna was even more determined. With one hefty arm round Mrs Bannister's shoulders and the other locked firmly about her frail, papery wrist she heaved her along. Joanna looked up and smiled when she saw Louisa May.

'Hello there, Lou. Young Dorothy and I are going down to the beach to freeze to death. Fancy coming?'

'OK.'

'Are you going to tell your mum? We'll be about an hour.'

Louisa May shook her head. 'She knows I'm out; she doesn't mind.'

'If you're sure.' Joanna gripped Dorothy's wrist more

firmly as they began to descend. 'Hold on to the banister, Mrs Bannister!' she ordered cheerfully.

Louisa May tugged irritably on her socks. They wilted instantly like rain-starved shrubs. At least she'd see the beach today; at least that part of the dream would come true.

Wathsea had never been a popular resort. Its beaches were more shingle than sand, its roads more sinewy than straight, so had never been able to compete with Skegness or Mablethorpe. None of which bothered Louisa May. She flung herself from one end of the beach to the other, running wildly into the sea one minute, crashing out of it the next. When she tired of that, she gazed in awe at a dead jellyfish marooned near the rocks, returning to the blob time and again.

'This is brilliant! Look at this! Look!'

'Anyone'd think you'd never seen the sea before!' Joanna laughed, amazed at Louisa May's reaction.

'I haven't,' Louisa May cried, stuffing shells into her pocket.

Joanna's smile faded. 'Never?'

'Well, only on telly and things, never in real life.'

'Not even for a day trip?'

'No. Look at this. Look at this!' She beckoned Joanna to where she was standing, ankles sinking in muddy sand. She pointed to where a dark green crab was desperately trying to return to its stone shelter which she had levered away. 'A crab, a real crab!'

Joanna looked, though not too closely. She preferred distance between herself and anything that nipped. 'Lou's found a crab, Mrs Bannister.' She waved to the sticklike figure who sat motionless at the foot of the cliff.

'Doesn't she like crabs?' Louisa May asked.

'Who knows, poor old love.'

Louisa May carefully lowered the slab back into place and stared across. 'What's wrong with her?'

'I think she's got something called Alzheimer's disease. It makes you forget things, even the names of people in your family.'

'Has she got a family?'

Joanna pulled her cardigan more tightly round her body. She shuddered. 'I don't know. I haven't been able to find out. I do know Wanda's supposed to take care of her and she gets an allowance for doing it, which is a laugh.'

'I don't like Mrs Putlock. I think she's a witch,' Louisa May confided.

Joanna snorted. 'Well, she does walk as if she's got a broomstick stuck up her jacksy but no, she's not a witch, Lou. Just don't let her get away with anything. You haven't let her have your giro, have you? That's her speciality, getting poor suckers to hand over their money.'

'Sort of, but we got it back.' Louisa May explained what had happened earlier.

Joanna grinned. 'Very canny. You've got a clever mum there, Lou.'

'Have I?' Louisa May had thought it was humiliating to have the cheque thrown back at them but Joanna made it sound like some well-thought-out plan.

'She'll leave you alone now she knows she can't pull a fast one.'

'I never looked at it like that.' Louisa May remembered how Georgette had said they would get the giro back all along. Joanna was right. She did have a 'canny' mother.

'Oh, Dorothy, stop! Don't eat that!' Joanna pelted towards Mrs Bannister, who was licking dollops of sand from the crevices of a rock. She stopped when Joanna reached her and scoured her mouth with the back of her hand. Joanna turned to Louisa May and shouted, 'We'd better call it a day. I'll see you after dinner. Come to my room and watch some TV.'

'OK,' Louisa May replied, running towards the jellyfish for one last prod.

Seven

Georgette smiled as she listened to Louisa May's breathless account of her time on the beach, touching her flushed cheek with the back of her hand.

'Then Mrs Bannister started eating sand; she's got Alka Seltzer's disease or something. Oh, yes, and dinner's earlier on a Saturday. Joanna says Wanda goes singing Country and Western in the Nag's Head so we have to eat at five.'

'The Nag's Head? How appropriate.'

'Can I watch telly in Joanna's room after? She invited me; I didn't ask.' Louisa May glanced at her mother. She still seemed tired and had dark shadows under her eyes. 'You don't mind, do you? I'll stay if you don't feel well,' she added.

Georgette shook her head and sat upright. 'No, I don't mind. First I'm going to have a bath and while I'm doing that you can unpack your clothes. They'll get fusty if you leave them in the carrier.'

Louisa May watched as her mother folded soap into the flannel.

'Won't be long,' Georgette said.

Louisa May's carrier bag was slumped on her side of the dressing table. She up-ended it into the middle of her bed and her clothes fell out heavily in one thick clump. She ruffled the clothes, which separated reluctantly, tingeing the air with mustiness. Two jumpers, three T-shirts, leggings, a shiny blue skirt which she loved but didn't fit any more, and a vest. That was it. The rest she was either wearing or it lay limply on top of the radiator.

What was there to do now? Nothing. Nothing at all. These were the times Louisa May hated—the long, empty times spent alone in dismal rooms. She knew she had to give herself another task before the gloom got to her. Catching sight of the kettle, she decided to make herself a cup of coffee. Even though she didn't like it much it would warm her up; it was chilly in the room and the radiator never seemed to come on.

The fox-fur dangled tiredly above the kettle, its beady eyes staring straight into the spout. Louisa May remembered the thirty pounds tucked safely away down its throat. Had Georgette stuffed the notes far down enough? If she hadn't, they might fall into the kettle, and get boiled away. She had better check. Her shoes depended upon it.

She perched on the edge of her mother's bed, the fur in her lap, and prodded inside. It was strange, sticking your fingers down an animal's throat, dead or not. She pulled gently. The folded money yielded easily and she placed it beside her. She listened for a second, in case her mother had finished in her bath, then delved again.

It was harder this time, her short fingers had to probe deeper, into a narrower hole. There was something. Paper again, but thicker than before. She pulled, easing the object bit by bit, until it reached the fox's mouth, yanking at what she could now see was a brown envelope, rolled into a tube. Louisa May flattened it and peered at the address.

Her breathing deepened. It was one of those letters from Wendy Almond, addressed to their basement room in Lincoln. The letters that Georgette had grown frozen-faced at receiving, the ones she'd refused to talk about or let Louisa May even look at. Strange she should have kept it, when all the others had been thrown away.

With trembling fingers, Louisa May turned the envelope over and slid out its contents. There was a white sheet of folded paper, and another, smaller letter. She opened the sheet. The address was in bold type, a Messrs Dimbleby and Partners, Solicitors. It was dated September 3rd—nearly two months ago.

'Dear Georgette Haddock,' it began, 'we have been instructed by our client, Mrs Wendy Almond, to contact you once again.

Mrs Almond is most anxious to establish communication with you in order to settle your estate. This is a matter of some urgency and we should appreciate an early response to this letter. Mrs Almond has included her own letter with this communication which explains the matter in more personal detail.

We urge you to telephone the office as soon as possible.'

There was a signature which began with a capital 'D' but tapered off into a squiggly black line. Louisa May didn't understand what the letter meant, exactly, but she sensed it was important.

She reached for the other, smaller envelope and turned it over in her hands. It had never been opened, although there was a well-thumbed tear at one corner, as if someone had begun to open it, then changed their mind.

She flipped it back. The front of the envelope simply had Georgette's name printed in the centre. In the distance, a door banged, and she heard voices. Quickly, she rammed the envelopes and money back into the fox's mouth and trailed it across the dresser where its eyes glazed over instantly with steam from the kettle.

She draped her clothes over the radiator then sat on her bed and waited for dinnertime.

Georgette and Louisa May hovered outside the dining room, the first to arrive and uncertain where to sit. Down the centre of the dining area, three tables had been pushed together and spread with mismatching and stained table cloths. The only other table was set into the alcove of the bay window. It had a cleaner looking cloth, as well as cruet set and sauce bottles.

'Shall we go in?' Louisa May asked. Georgette fidgeted nervously with the neck of her jumper, putting Louisa May on edge.

'Are you sure you got the time right?'

'I think so. We could sit there. We might see the sea from over there.' She pointed to the table in the bay window.

'You'll do no such thing!' Wanda pushed past brusquely, knocking Louisa May against the door frame. She stalked over to the table in question, brushing away imaginary crumbs from the cloth. She then laid out the cutlery she'd been carrying, making sure the knife and fork were precisely positioned. 'This is Mr Deacon's place, reserved for him at all times. He pays full board and lodging, you see. He works for a living, doesn't believe the state owes him one like some. You sit over there. Mr Putlock'll be in in a minute with your meal.' The landlady departed without another glance.

They chose seats at the far end, nearest the wall. A good place for the have-nots, Louisa May thought. Georgette was restless. She kept rubbing her forehead and staring blankly at the tablecloth. 'Are you OK?' Louisa May asked.

'Fine, just a bit hot, that's all.'

'Hot? It's freezing in here.'

'Well, I'm hot.'

'You said you wouldn't play the game again for a while.'

'I'm not playing games, Louisa May. I only said I was hot.'

Mr Putlock thrust his bristly face around the door, stared, then disappeared. Seconds later he bustled in, a plate in each hand. He squeezed between Louisa May and her mother, parting them with his black hairy arms. Louisa May scowled as his thumb stuck, snail-like, and transferred a grey, greasy print to the rim of her plate. 'Tea's coming,' he said gruffly, and left.

Louisa May examined her meal. Sausages and beans. She prodded a sausage with her fork and it oozed a stream of liquid fat, making her feel queasy. The underside of her meat was over-done, burned and charcoal-black. The upperside, bright pink and fleshy. Her beans did not move as she shovelled beneath them, but stayed in a glutinous clump as her clothes had done when she'd emptied them on to her bed.

Louisa May was hungry. She knew there'd be nothing else to eat and that this was better than nothing. Blocking her nose against the taste she took her first mouthful.

Ambrose returned, clattering teapots and cups on a tray. These were delivered in front of them without comment. No pudding then, Louisa May guessed. She cut into her sausage and thought it was probably a good job. Georgette didn't even try. Her food solidified, untouched on her plate, which she pushed to one side.

She poured the tea from a leaky stainless steel pot, unable to stop half the liquid from dripping on to the tablecloth. Tiredly, she edged one cup towards Louisa May and curved her hands round her own, staring vacantly into the brown water.

Louisa May heard voices on the stairs and knew Joanna was trying to persuade Mrs Bannister to follow her again. 'Come on,' she could hear her saying. 'You need to eat.'

'That sounds like Joanna, Mum. You'll like her, she's nice.'

Joanna entered and grinned at both of them. 'Sausage and beans, what a change! It must be, oh, at least two days since we've had sausage and beans!' she said, guiding Mrs Bannister into the seat opposite Georgette. Joanna held out her hand for Georgette to shake but Georgette just stared at her over the edge of her cup. The younger woman took her hand away but continued to smile.

'I'm Joanna, but please call me Coconut, if you prefer.' She winked at Louisa May then tried again with Georgette. 'Are you settling in OK? It's not much of a place, is it, Wathsea?'

Georgette looked up and shrugged. 'Everywhere seems the same to me,' she said in a flat voice.

'Oh, no. I went to university in Manchester and that's nothing like here. Manchester's full of life and character and—'

'It depends *how* you're living, not *where* you're living. As I said, everywhere seems the same to me.'

'Oh. Well, I suppose so. I understand you've moved around a lot.'

'You could say that.'

'It's hard, isn't it, not having roots?'

Georgette looked searchingly into Joanna's face but didn't reply. Ambrose bustled in with two more plates of beans and sausages. He slammed them down in front of the new arrivals. 'Watch her with it,' he commanded, signalling towards Mrs Bannister.

'She'll be all right,' Joanna replied. Ambrose grunted and hurried out. 'Come on, Mrs B. Look at this lovely meal.' She began cutting into Mrs Bannister's sausages, which were equally as black and disgusting as Louisa May's had been. But Mrs Bannister gazed into space even when Joanna held a piece of the sausage up towards her mouth.

'Doesn't she want it?' Louisa May asked.

'Who in their right minds would? Come on, Mrs B., just one mouthful.'

Unfortunately, Ambrose chose the same moment to thump down the stainless steel teapot as Mrs Bannister showed her helper what she could do with her 'one mouthful'. Her arm swept across the cloth like a windscreen wiper, clearing her plate and the teapot in a wild swoop. The hot liquid hovered in the air, a sheet of transparent toffee, for what seemed like a whole minute before it landed, scalding hot, over Ambrose. He screamed, clutching his burnt arm in anguish. 'Ooh! Ahhh! Ohh!'

On cue Wanda rushed in, her hair shaking perilously like a jelly about to topple. 'What's going on? What's happening?'

'I'm scarred for life, that's all. Look! Look! Prob'ly third degree burns those. Ohh!' The afflicted man held out his wound for his wife to see.

She barely glanced at it. 'Never mind your daft arm. What about all this mess? Beans and tea everywhere. They're impossible to shift, bean stains. Get stuck in the tufts.' She turned to where Mrs Bannister sat, passively watching the commotion like a bored bystander.

44

'I'll need some cream on this arm,' Ambrose wailed childishly. 'It was hot, that tea.'

'Well, it's supposed to be, you daft 'a'porth. Go rub some marg on it,' his wife retorted.

Ambrose shuffled out, still clutching his arm and muttering about hospitals. Wanda waved the dishcloth near to Mrs Bannister's face. 'I'm fed up of you. You're more bother than you're worth, you old bag!'

Joanna chewed her sausage lazily. 'Keep your wig on, Wanda. She didn't mean any harm.'

Wanda pouted. 'Never mind my wig, Miss High-and-Mighty-never-done-a-day's-work-in-her-life—'

Louisa May held her breath as Joanna sprang to her feet, forked sausage still in hand.

'Don't lecture me about hard work! You've never spent three years of your life cramming for exams until you don't know whether you're coming or going. Though I suppose that doesn't count "on account of it bein' educashunal".'

Louisa May giggled at Joanna's impersonation. Wanda glowered, her spite turned fully in the graduate's direction now, which, Louisa May realized, was exactly as Joanna had planned it. 'Having brains hasn't got you very far, 'as it? I don't care what those women libbers say; I'd rather have a nice figure than all the degrees in China, I would.' Wanda scanned Joanna's round frame to press home her point.

'Well,' Joanna fired back, 'seeing as you haven't got either your life must be a complete misery!'

Louisa May could not believe how Joanna was answering back. If she carried on . . . a brief, sidelong glance told her that Georgette didn't seem to be listening at all. If she had, Louisa May would not have been allowed to watch television with 'such a rude person'.

'I'll show you what misery is!' Wanda growled, her dishcloth raised as if to throw it at her tenant.

'Go on, then!' Joanna dared. 'And I'll be on that phone so quick—'

Louisa May gaped as Mrs Putlock took aim but the landlady was forced to hold her pose as a new voice cut in to the drama. 'Ah, Wanda! Party time. Let me guess: Musical Statues?'

As if magnetized, all heads turned towards the door. Only Georgette stayed as she was, her hands stiffening around her tea-cup.

Eight

The expression on Wanda's face changed faster than the waves in the sea. 'Why, Mr Deacon! You're back early. I 'aven't even thought of your dinner yet.'

Stephen Deacon grinned. 'Time off for good behaviour, Mrs P.'

Wanda fluttered her eyelids several times. 'I've got some nice steak in the fridge. Won't take me two minutes to grill.'

'Steak! You know the way to a man's heart, Wanda, you really do.'

He strode confidently to the table by the window and sat down. Wanda hurried over, rubbing the already clean surface with the all-purpose dishcloth.

'I can make you a jacket potato in the microwave,' she fussed, 'and some fried mushrooms. I know you love fried mushrooms.'

'Great. Have you done something to your hair, Wanda?' he asked.

She patted it. 'Honey blonde, like Dolly Parton's. What do you think?'

Everyone in the room seemed to wait for his answer.

'It really . . . suits you,' he said seriously.

He must be blind, Louisa May thought, but Wanda beamed.

'I'll go get your steak ready.'

She sauntered towards the door, then turned to the occupants of the centre tables. 'If the rest of you 'ave finished, I'm sure Mr Deacon would like to eat his 'ard-earned meal in peace.' She smiled sweetly but pointedly at them and left.

'Please don't go on my account, any of you,' he said casually.

Nobody replied but Louisa May swivelled round.

'Do you remember me?' she blurted out, surprised at herself for asking, but she couldn't help it. It was him, this Mr Deacon, the assistant from Batty's. He was fussing with his tie, but stopped when she spoke and glanced at her.

'Were you in the shop earlier?' he asked uncertainly. Louisa May nodded.

His face brightened. 'Of course I remember. You were with that extraordinary woman.'

'That was my mum.'

'Where is she now?' he asked.

'Here.' She tugged at Georgette's jumper. To Louisa May's dismay the assistant left his chair and came towards them.

He was a shiny man. His hair was shiny and his teeth were shiny and his eyes were shiny. And of course his shoes; his shoes were extremely shiny.

He stood next to Georgette and leaned forwards, holding out his hand. 'Stephen Deacon, nephew of Samuel Batty, shoe shop owner. I'm delighted to make your acquaintance.'

Georgette frowned while Louisa May willed her to be normal.

'You looked so . . . ' he paused, as if searching for an exact description . . . 'so astonishing this morning, so ethereal. I thought you were an actress or something.'

Georgette glowered at him from the rim of her teacup.

'No, young man, I am neither an actress nor a dance

hall floozy and it would please me if you would kindly not address me so directly in future.'

Louisa May sighed. Rosanna was back but Stephen Deacon seemed thrilled.

'You are an actress!' He gently bent over and kissed the back of her hand.

'And you are forward, sir!' She snatched back her hand as if it had been bitten and glared angrily at Stephen, who continued to beam at her admiringly.

Pulling an empty chair from nearby he perched on the edge of it, facing Georgette. 'Fantastic! Are you into the Method?'

Georgette raised her enquiring eyebrow.

'You must be,' he continued, 'or something similar, where you have to live your part every minute of the day, even when you're not on stage? Brilliant! I'm a bit of a frustrated actor myself. Who were you this morning? Someone out of Jane Austen?'

Louisa May gaped. He really thought her mother was an actress. An actress! 'She's not—' Louisa May began, but Georgette swiftly interrupted her.

'Not now, dear. Why don't you help your friend? She seems to be struggling somewhat. And then did you say you had been invited to Miss Frankish's for charades this evening?'

'But, Mum—'

'I could do with a hand,' 'Miss Frankish' said, wrestling with Mrs Bannister who was twisting out from her grip like a bad-tempered toddler.

'Have you seen my Emerald?' the old lady whined at Mr Deacon. 'Or my Pearl?'

'Of course not, dear, but the moment I do I'll let you know,' he said, winking at Georgette.

'Will you be all right?' Louisa May asked her mother,

not moving. A little while ago, Georgette had been coughing and feeling hot. Perhaps she needed her to stay, just in case.

'Of course she's going to be all right,' Mr Deacon exclaimed. 'This delightful lady is going to join me for supper, I hope, if I'm not being too forward, Miss . . . Mrs . . . ?' He paused expectantly.

'*Ms* Van Der Lees. Rosanna,' Georgette replied.

'Rosanna,' he repeated.

'I'd be delighted.'

Louisa May felt uneasy. Her mother had never mixed with anyone before, especially not a man. It had just never happened. Her heart had always remained true to Daniel Brody, her first and only love. Yet here she was, being escorted by this near-stranger to his table. Not only that, she was nodding and smiling and shaking her head as if she'd known this bloke all her life.

Then Wanda came bustling through, flustered but trying not to seem it. 'Oh, Mr Deacon, I am ever so sorry but Ambrose has—' She stopped, mid-sentence, at the sight of Georgette at Mr Deacon's table, snapping out, 'Oh, Mr Deacon, she can't sit there!'

'Why ever not?' he asked calmly.

'Well, she's not . . . she's not a full-board customer like you are, Mr Deacon. She's a . . . social case. Middle table. Middle table.'

'Can't you bend the rules just this once?' He leaned his head to one side, like a puppy. 'And I am giving you a lift to the Nag's Head.'

'Oh, all right.' The landlady shot Georgette a venomous look before turning and abruptly leaving the room.

'It's all that hair dye she uses. The chemicals make her bad-tempered,' Stephen said in a loud whisper.

'Dyed hair does so age a woman,' Georgette agreed. She turned to face her daughter with eyes which were bright and clear for the first time in weeks.

'Back by nine, not a minute later, darling.'

Nine? Louisa May was amazed. That was three hours away. She didn't usually allow her to be gone for three minutes, let alone three hours.

Louisa May's concern evaporated into excitement and she smiled brightly. Three hours of television. Excellent! And it was not as if Georgette was going anywhere; she was only a staircase away.

Before turning quickly to catch Joanna, Louisa May curtsied prettily for her mother. 'Have a pleasant evening, Mama!' she yelled cheekily.

Upstairs, Joanna closed Mrs Bannister's door firmly behind her, then pointed her thumb at the door opposite.

'That's his room, Sneaky Deacon's.'

'Don't you like him?'

'Not much.'

'Why?'

'He's a bit of a creep. Didn't you notice how he introduced himself as Batty's nephew? Couldn't leave that out, could he? Just because his uncle owns a shop. Big deal! I'd warn your mum not to get too close to him, if I were you.'

'She's not getting close to him!'

Joanna smirked good-humouredly. 'Well, she's getting closer to him than I ever managed. I asked him out for a curry once and he turned me down flat.'

'He was nice to me in the shop.'

''Course he was. He's on commission; gets a bonus for every pair of shoes he sells.'

'Oh.' Louisa May felt disappointed, she'd been willing to like the shiny man, especially as he'd made her mother look happy.

'But he must be special if he's the only one allowed to sit next to the window.'

Joanna laughed. 'That doesn't make him special. Wanda fancies him like mad, that's all. It drives Ambrose potty. You watch next mealtime—it'll take your mind off the salmonella sausages.'

'My mum will be all right with Mr Deacon, won't she?' Louisa May asked, wondering what all this 'getting close' business meant.

Joanna laughed again and unlocked the door to her room, leaving Louisa May to follow. ''Course she will. Now back to more important things,' she declared, delving inside her bedside cabinet. 'As neither of us has got a date for the evening, you and me have got some serious pigging-out to do! Come in. Take a pew.' She pointed to her bed and returned to foraging about in the cupboard. Louisa May closed the door behind her and sat down.

The room was much smaller than theirs, but cosier. No thin orange coverlets here but a thick, quilted duvet covered in bright green and red stripes. In the alcove a bookcase full of books and cassettes and videos hid Joanna's damp wall. This, together with the new-looking television set and the warmth from a fan heater, made Louisa May feel as if she was in a real bedroom, like in magazines.

'You've got a lot of lovely things,' Louisa May commented, reaching out to touch a teddy bear perched on top of a pillow.

The reply was muffled. 'Oh, yes, well, that's what you get when your mother decides to run off to Australia:

lots of lovely things to stop her feeling guilty. I've even got a car. How's that for guilt? Here, why don't you help yourself?' Joanna emerged from her cupboard with a packet of walnut muffins and indicated that Louisa May should choose her own.

More than willingly, she slipped off the bed and knelt down. It was like a supermarket shelf inside; multipacks of chocolate bars lay piled on top of each other, squashed into place by slab cakes and family packets of tea-time assortment. 'Wow! Can I have any?'

''Course you can. You're the guest.' It was difficult pulling out the cakes without everything else falling. Suddenly an avalanche of cellophaned treats slid into Louisa May's lap, followed by a metallic object.

'What's this?' she asked. Joanna squinted.

'My mobile phone. Shove it right to the back. Don't want Wanda Woollyknickers finding it.'

Louisa May did as she was told and emerged with a packet of ginger nuts. 'You eat a lot, Joanna.'

'Listen, Tin Ribs, I have to eat to stay sane. There's nothing wrong in coping with life through a haze of hazelnut shortcake and lemon puffs. In those immortal words of the great philosopher, St John of the Lennons, ''Whatever gets you through the night''.'

Louisa May nibbled thoughtfully on her biscuit. 'Mum and me pretend we're posh people from the olden days. She's someone called Rosanna Van Der Lees and I'm her daughter. We travel from place to place having adventures. When we came here we were returning from a safari holiday in Africa, where we'd hunted wild beasts and nearly been eaten by cannibals.'

'And where had you come from really?'

'Near the crisp factory in Lincoln.'

Joanna snorted, spraying crumbs everywhere. 'So that's what the "dance hall floozy" bit was all about? I did wonder.'

Louisa May confided, 'I get embarrassed sometimes, when she does it in front of people. It's like she can't stop pretending.'

'Well, don't be embarrassed. There's nothing wrong with using your imagination; it's creative. And she's doing a good job with you. How old are you?'

'Nearly ten.'

'Hmm. Some of the kids who've stayed here have been right little swines. Even those money-grabbers downstairs won't take families in any more. I'm surprised you were allowed over the threshold. Glad though.'

'So no kid's ever been in here?'

Joanna grimaced. 'I don't share my ginger nuts with just anybody, you know!'

Louisa May beamed proudly. Joanna thought she was normal. Normal enough to allow her into her room. Normal enough to play with her on the beach. Joanna was the first person who had said something nice about her pretend games with Georgette. At school, she had often been teased by other children about her mother's odd clothes and even odder mannerisms. 'You're not normal,' they were always telling her. Well, they were wrong. Louisa May struggled to say something to her heroine but the words stuck shyly to her tongue. Instead she sat back and watched as Joanna switched on the TV set.

A blond-haired man was splashing about in a river, fighting an enormous crocodile that anyone could tell was made out of rubber. 'Stay still, ya bleeder,' the man commanded.

'Drop dead, Aussie,' Joanna commanded, punching the remote control. Instantly the picture changed.

Louisa May glanced at her friend and remembered what she had said about her mother being in Australia. 'Has your mum been away long?' she asked.

Joanna sank her teeth into her second walnut muffin. 'Two years.'

Louisa May couldn't imagine being without Georgette for more than a day. 'Don't you miss her?'

'I'm a big girl now,' she replied.

'What about your dad? Where's he?'

'Here, there, and everywhere. He's in the air force. I don't see him much, either.'

'Oh. That's sad.'

'Not really. As long as he keeps sending me my muffin money, I'll survive!' Although the words were spoken lightly, there was a sadness behind them which Louisa May recognized. She used the same tone herself when people asked her about Daniel Brody, pretending it didn't matter he was not around when it did. Not knowing what else to do, she held out the packet of biscuits.

'Ginger nut?' she asked.

'Tin ribs!' Joanna joked back.

'Coconut head!' Louisa May responded, giggling.

'I must warn you, girlie, I'm good at this. I have a degree in Geography and name-calling!'

'Muffin face!' Louisa May challenged.

'I can't believe a kid called Haddock is daring to call me names but there you go . . . ' She rubbed her hands together with glee.

When Georgette collected Louisa May she found her not glued to the television as she had expected, but surrounded by strips and strips of paper, her eyes red and dry from laughter.

'Mum!' Louisa May cried, waving one of the strips in the air. 'Joanna's taught me to do anagrams. Did you know she's a "rank fish"? and "I am a lousy cod"? That one's from my name but I haven't finished it yet. You're a "dead hot rocket egg".'

A faint smile drifted across Georgette's lips but Louisa May noticed instantly the shadows beneath her eyes had deepened since the meal. Immediately, Louisa May rose, conscious of her mother's need to be in her own room.

'What do you say to Miss Frankish?' Georgette prompted.

Louisa May turned and grinned, 'Thanks for having me, "Rank fish"!'

Nine

Louisa May became a regular visitor to Joanna's room. As schools were on half-term it gave her a week in which to play on the beach and watch television. The beach always thrilled her because each time she went, it changed. If the tide was in, she fought with the waves, daring herself to jump into the icy-cold water. If the tide was out, she traipsed along the new land left behind by the sea, searching for shells and strange stones which she would wash in the sink when she returned to her room.

Georgette never came out, postponing everything, including buying Louisa May's shoes, until school started. She stayed in bed most of the day, reading or just staring into space. The coughing had worsened, so that Louisa May was made to go to the corner shop every other day for more toilet rolls.

Only in the evenings did Georgette come alive, when she would dress herself carefully for dinner and wait patiently at the middle table until Stephen Deacon entered and escorted her to his place by the window.

Wanda suffered in silence, wearing more and more make-up as she served her paying guest his meal whilst trying to ignore his companion totally. It drove her mad that she couldn't punish Georgette by refusing to bring her food across; Georgette rarely ate more than a mouthful of whatever was put in front of her.

Ambrose, on the other hand, was almost pleasant, despite his over-bandaged arm. It seemed he was glad 'that Deacon bloke' had 'taken a shine to Mrs Haddock' as he was fond of reminding his wife. He whistled as he dished up an assortment of diabolical but filling meals, winking occasionally at Louisa May as he gave her extra helpings.

'Teacher's pet,' Joanna would tease, pinching a chip.

Louisa May began to relax and by the following Saturday she had decided that she liked Wathsea even better than Lincoln. There hadn't been a Joanna in Lincoln.

It was lunchtime. Louisa May's stomach rumbled as she watched Georgette combing her hair and scowling every time the comb struck the tangled strands at the bottom, yanking at her scalp.

'Joanna doesn't have that problem. She doesn't need a brush or anything,' Louisa May observed.

Georgette's scowl deepened. 'Well, she wouldn't, would she, being almost bald.'

Louisa May blinked. It was unusual for Georgette to be unkind to anyone.

'She says short hair's easier to manage when there's no shower.'

'I wouldn't know.'

'She says—'

Georgette tossed the comb at the dressing table where it ricocheted off the kettle with a metallic clang. 'Do we have to talk about Joanna all the time? I know the fact that she possesses a television makes her a goddess in your eyes but there are other people in the world, you know.'

Louisa May stared in surprise at the comb. 'I was only saying. There's no need to throw a wobbly.'

Georgette opened her mouth to speak, then her shoulders sagged as she glanced sorrowfully at her daughter. 'I'm sorry, Louisa May. I know you're fond of

Joanna but she just seems a bit too good to be true at times. Let's change the subject, eh?'

'OK,' Louisa May agreed readily. 'When are we going for my shoes? You said Saturday and Sneaky Deaky—'

'Mr Deacon.'

'Whatever. He'll be working in the shop. We might get them cheap.'

Georgette blushed. Louisa May, thinking it was because she'd mentioned Stephen Deacon's name, began to tease her. 'Your eyes can meet over the wellingtons and as you move forward to give him your ticket his hand accidentally touches yours. Your heart races. Then, Daniel Brody suddenly appears at the door, a rose in one hand, diamond ring in the other. He falls to his knees and cries, "Georgette, Georgette, you must choose." Then—'

'Louisa May.'

'Yes, Mama?' Louisa May beamed, hoping her mother would join in with the game, wanting her to end the story where she, Daniel Brody, and their little miracle, Louisa May, sail off into the sunset.

'Pass me the toilet roll.'

Sighing, Louisa May did as asked. In robotic fashion she tore off strips of paper for Georgette to cough into, waiting a few seconds at a time for her mother to screw each segment into a tight ball after she'd used it.

'I wish you'd get some medicine. You've had that cough for ages now.'

Georgette patted the bed, waiting for Louisa May to sit down. 'We can't get your shoes today, I've—'

Louisa May interrupted, prepared for any excuse. 'Joanna says she'll take me. She says she's going into Wathsea anyway and it'd be no trouble. I told her you might not feel well enough . . . '

Georgette's blush deepened. 'It's not that. I haven't got the money . . . I've lent it to Mr Deacon.'

Louisa May's eyes darted towards the fox-fur. 'Lent it? Why? He's not a have-not!'

'But he only gets paid monthly and his uncle's awfully mean . . . '

'But it was for my shoes.'

'If you'll just listen,' Georgette pleaded. 'He's invited me out for a meal. Instead of sitting with that stupid woman ogling him all the time, he said wouldn't it be nice if . . . Oh, Louisa May, I've never had a meal out with anyone before.'

Louisa May folded her arms and stared at the sink.

'You don't even eat. It'll be a waste of money and you keep saying you're not well. You never let me go out if I'm not well. You'd tell me to stay in and drink bucketfuls of that orange stuff that takes forever to come out of the bottle.'

'It's once, Louisa May, just once.'

'You'll be running off to Australia with him next,' she mumbled, refusing to speak for the rest of the afternoon.

At seven o'clock, Stephen Deacon knocked loudly on the door. Louisa May opened it reluctantly, her sour expression not budging an inch, despite his outfit. He was dressed in top hat and tails and looked ridiculous.

'What do you think?' he asked, bowing low.

'I think your rabbit's escaped,' she replied, leaving the door open and returning to her sulking position on the bed. Georgette swept past, decked out in every bead and bracelet and hat pin she possessed in the world, the fox-fur bobbing frantically against her bony chest.

Stephen's eyes widened. 'Rosanna, you look splendid!'

'Gilbert! How handsome you are!'

'Gilbert?' Louisa May enquired.

Georgette smiled. 'Yes, I have my Gilbert with me once again.'

'I'd watch it, then, if I were you, "Gilbert", you've been killed three times already.'

He stared at Louisa May blankly for a second before turning to Georgette, holding out his elbow for her to take.

'We'll be back by nine, won't we, Gilbert?' 'Rosanna' enquired.

'On the dot.'

Georgette bent to kiss Louisa May, wheezing slightly as her lips brushed her daughter's ear.

'Make sure you've got your bog roll,' Louisa May advised.

It didn't feel the same at Joanna's that night. Louisa May couldn't settle, knowing Georgette was out of the hotel. Even when Joanna called Stephen Deacon all the worst swear words she'd ever heard for borrowing the shoe money, she still couldn't cheer up. By the time the Nine O'Clock News came on, Louisa May was perched on the edge of Joanna's bed, facing the door.

'A watched pot never boils,' Joanna informed her. By half-past nine, Louisa May was peering outside, listening for any signs of arrivals downstairs.

'She's late,' Louisa May said worriedly. Joanna yawned.

'Stop fussing. Your mum must have been out with people before.'

'She hasn't. She's supposed to be waiting for Daniel Brody.'

'Ah! The mysterious Capt'n Brody,' Joanna teased.

Louisa May didn't reply. She was half-way out of the door again.

'Come and watch the funny bit at the end of the news. You're letting a draught in,' Joanna ordered.

Louisa May obeyed reluctantly. It was the only part of the programme she ever listened to properly. Perhaps it would take her mind off Georgette.

'It could only happen in America,' began the newsreader cheerfully. 'A multi-millionairess from Baltimore, Mrs Connie Melushi, has left her entire estate to her pet pig Penrose. Penrose, a Vietnamese pot-belly, is worth an estimated fifty-three million dollars. Let's hope he has a swill time with it! That's all from us. Have a pleasant evening.'

'Joanna?' Louisa May asked.

'Mmm?'

'What's an estate?'

'Your estate means everything you own, so if I left you my estate you'd have three teddies, a quilt cover, and a cupboard full of biscuits.'

'Oh.' Louisa May fell silent. The letter in the fox-fur had mentioned an estate and she hadn't known what it meant. She tried to remember the exact wording. 'Contact us as soon as possible with regards to your estate.' Did that mean Georgette had an estate? Maybe they were rich? Maybe someone had left fifty-three million dollars to them instead of a pot-bellied pig. Louisa May's mind raced, teeming with possibilities, her mother's bad time-keeping almost forgotten. 'Joanna?'

'That's my name—don't wear it out.'

'If you hated somebody but they wanted to give you an estate, what would you do?'

Joanna scratched her leg. 'No problem there. I'd decide it was my Christian duty to forgive and forget and turn the other cheek at the same time.'

'Even if they were Australian?'

Joanna laughed. 'Lou, I'd eat kangaroo burgers and sing "Waltzing Matilda" all day long!' She reached out and grabbed Louisa May's wrists and swung her round the room, barely missing the television set. Louisa May's shrieks drowned out Georgette's quiet knocking. It was only when the door opened a fraction that Joanna dropped Louisa May into a heap on the floor.

'I'm sorry I'm late,' Georgette said, her voice low and breathless. She gazed at Louisa May's flushed cheeks and wild hair for a moment then disappeared. Louisa May scrambled up from the floor and gave Joanna a hug.

'Thanks for looking after me, Joanna. I think you're great.'

Joanna patted her admirer's cheek and said goodnight but her concerned eyes had followed Georgette, not Louisa May, out of the door.

Georgette was already in bed, her clothes discarded in an untidy heap, the fox-fur slung across them as if to guard its lair.

'Did you have a nice time?' Louisa May asked, kicking off her shoes and socks. 'Did you manage to save any money?' she added quietly.

'Just turn the light out, darling, I'm tired. I'll tell you all about it in the morning.'

Louisa May crept into bed, disappointed. She'd been hoping to bring the small matter of fifty-three million dollars into the conversation somehow.

She couldn't sleep. She'd tried counting sheep but a massive fox kept chasing after them. Then she remembered Penrose, the pot-bellied pig, and tried to work out what 'pot-bellied' pigs looked like. Then she thought of Wendy Almond.

Secretly, she thought Wendy Almond was a nice name, but she would never have dared to say so. In the end, she sat up in the darkness and sighed.

'Mum, can I sleep with you?' she asked. Turning back her covers, she made the journey across in one stride. Georgette groaned but didn't answer. Louisa May reached out her hand so she could gauge a space for herself. Her fingers met with Georgette's shoulder. It felt hot and sticky-wet. She pressed lightly on other parts of her mother's back and arm; all the same. Hot and clammy.

More urgently, she touched her mother's skin, her neck, the side of her face. She was burning. Strands of hair stuck rigidly to the skin which she knew would hurt if she tried to pull them away. 'Mum, Mum,' Louisa May whispered, 'Mum, Mum, wake up, you're boiling.'

Georgette curled tightly into herself. She was shivering, despite the heat her body gave out. And her breathing was low and rasping as if every breath had to pass over sandpaper before leaving her mouth.

Alarmed and confused, Louisa May tried to think. Did they have any medicine? Even that orange stuff for children might be better than nothing. She couldn't remember if they had any left.

Climbing out of bed, she fumbled about in the dressing table. Nothing but books and old clothes. Her mother's handbag was just full of rubbish and her purse . . . her purse was empty. Reluctantly, she clambered back into

Georgette's bed. She hated the feel of her damp T-shirt pressing into her but she clung on to it all the same.

Closing her eyes, she told herself that everything would be all right in the morning. Georgette would get up and tell her all about her meal out and then they'd go down to the beach. The sea air was supposed to be good for people. That's what they'd do. They'd go down to the beach and watch the seagulls diving at the waves. Maybe there'd be a jellyfish or crabs. And when they got back, the cough would have gone and everything would be brilliant.

Ten

Louisa May awoke, stiff and cramped from her fitful sleep. She turned and gently touched her mother's shoulder, hoping this time it would be cool and dry. But it wasn't. She was even hotter than during the night. 'Mum, Mum,' Louisa May whispered urgently. Georgette didn't respond. All her energy seemed to be focused on breathing those short, rasping breaths which filled Louisa May with panic.

'Mum, wake up, please!' She leaned over to look into her mother's face but it was buried deeply into the pillow, hidden by matted hair.

'I'm going to get Joanna. She'll know what to do.'

From the doorway, a bleary-eyed Joanna diagnosed flu. 'I thought she looked ill last night. I'll call a doctor.' Half an hour later she reappeared, running agitated fingers through her stubbly hair.

'No one will come. You're not registered and they won't make house calls on Sundays except in emergencies.'

Louisa May's eyes filled with tears. 'But this is an emergency. It's not flu. She's had flu loads of times and it's not like this.'

Georgette had burrowed beneath the covers like a frightened animal. Every few seconds her body stiffened as the pain gripped her lungs with its steel fingers. Joanna realized Louisa May was right; this was much worse than flu.

Trying not to scare her, she spoke calmly, hiding her own concern. 'There's probably some new bug going round Wathsea. We'll go to the hospital; they'll sort her out. I'll bring my car round and you fetch Deaky to help me carry her down the stairs. OK?'

Louisa May nodded, snatching a glance at Georgette before running down the corridor to his room. She banged and pounded on his door, but there was no reply. Desperately, she twisted the handle and peered inside. The smell of sweaty socks hit her, followed by the sound of heavy snoring.

'Mr Deacon! Mr Deacon!' The snoring stopped then started again. Striding to his bed, she shook the sleeping body beneath the covers. 'Mr Deacon, you have to help!'

At last Stephen Deacon woke, startled at the sight of Louisa May's anxious face bearing down on him. 'What is it?' he asked gruffly, yanking his blankets above his chin.

'Mum's ill. We need you to help.'

'Help?'

'Take her to the hospital.'

He scowled at his watch. 'Eight o'clock! Tch! Here, give her two of these.' Reaching out, he groped for a white plastic tub on his dressing table.

'But she's hot and sweaty,' Louisa May pleaded, 'they won't help.'

'Listen, kid, Sunday's my only lie-in of the week. I've got stocktaking all afternoon. Tell Rosa—tell Georgette I'll see her tonight.'

'But . . .'

He pulled his pillow over his head, instructing her to close the door after herself. Fighting back her tears, she returned to her room where Joanna was trying to lift

Georgette into an upright position but the sick woman's weight defeated her. 'I'll have to drag her down the stairs at this rate,' she announced tensely.

Louisa May bit into her lip. 'I'm going to get Mr P.,' she said, dashing from the room.

'Fat lot of good that'll do,' Joanna yelled after her.

Ambrose was in the kitchen, funnelling vinegar into tomato sauce bottles. 'You're back quick. Told you there's no buses at this time,' he said grumpily, without looking up.

Louisa May swallowed hard. 'Mr Putlock, it's me, from room five.'

The landlord stopped pouring and scowled. 'What do you want? Residents aren't allowed in here, specially kids.'

'I know but it's important. My mum's got to go to hospital and Joanna can't carry her down the stairs.'

'Why not? She's big enough!' He laughed at his crude remark and wiped the rim of the ketchup bottle with his finger.

Louisa May felt her panic boil over into anger. 'That's not funny! We need help and you're just laughing and Stephen Deacon's a lazy pig!'

'What's that wet wazzock got to do with anything?'

'He won't help either. He's gone back to sleep.'

'Phh! Best place for him, away from other men's wives . . . where is she? I'll soon sort her out.'

Louisa May followed the landlord up the stairs and into their room where he scooped Georgette up as if she was a bag of popcorn. 'It's a good job Wanda's set off to her mother's. She won't be best pleased by all this,' he mumbled, hurrying down the stairs and out to the roadside where Joanna had parked. He bent awkwardly to lever his cargo on to the back seat. 'She's all skin and bone.'

'Thank you for your expert medical opinion,' Joanna said, twisting the key in the ignition. He stared begrudgingly at her before ambling back into the hotel. 'All set?' she asked, smiling at Louisa May, who was cradling Georgette's head in her lap.

'All set,' came the distant reply.

The Staff Nurse on duty at Wathsea Infirmary wasn't going to see them at first. 'We're only a cottage hospital; we don't have a casualty department,' she explained. When Joanna, angrier than Louisa May had ever seen her, shouted that the headlines 'Hospital Refuses To Help Sick Woman With Child' would not look very impressive in the *Wathsea Advertiser*, the Staff Nurse agreed to have 'a quick look' at Georgette.

The 'quick look' lasted the rest of the morning. Louisa May and Joanna waited as first one doctor then another disappeared behind a flowery partition.

There were many hushed conversations which Louisa May ached to understand but couldn't. Joanna stretched out her hand and folded Louisa May's small, cold fingers inside it. 'It'll be all right,' she mouthed.

Louisa May stared numbly into space. She did not believe her. Eventually another Staff Nurse, Staff Nurse Rook, led them along the corridor to her office. 'I need a few details from you,' she called over her navy blue shoulder, walking briskly away.

Reluctantly, Louisa May followed, with Joanna gabbling frantically in her ear. 'Listen, Lou, I'm your Auntie Joanna, right? Just play along with anything I say.'

Louisa May nodded, only half-listening, glancing first towards the now-distant flowery curtains, before shuffling into the office.

Half an hour later, Staff Nurse Rook read back the details, some true and some false, which Joanna and Louisa May had given her. 'Your mother's name is Georgette Haddock and she's twenty-seven years old. You're in Wathsea on holiday with your auntie, who is your mother's twin sister.' Here the nurse paused, glanced at Joanna's rotund features, then continued. 'You're all staying at Cliff Top Villas Hotel during the half-term holidays and had planned to return later today to . . .'

'Manchester.'

'Lincoln.'

'Which one?'

Joanna laughed lightly. 'I live in Manchester but sis lives in Lincoln. Wathsea's like half-way. We don't see each other that often . . . although we're very close. Like this.' She crossed her fingers to emphasize the point.

'I see.' Staff Nurse Rook then asked questions about how long Georgette had been coughing and what the house was like in Lincoln. Louisa May answered honestly, but each answer seemed to bring on another question until her head ached.

'Can I see my mum, now?' she begged.

The nurse tapped her pen on her desk, seeming deep in thought. 'I'll go find out. If you'd just wait here for a minute.'

Louisa May groaned. This time, though, a minute meant a minute, and the nurse returned almost immediately with one of the doctors. The doctor's concerned eyes darted from one person in the room to another. Louisa May thought the worst. 'She's dead, isn't she?' she cried out.

The doctor shook her head vigorously. 'No, she's in no danger of dying at all.' Louisa May felt her whole body slump as the doctor quickly continued, 'But Mrs Haddock needs to be transferred to Kesteven Infirmary immediately; they have better facilities there to run tests and treat chest problems.'

'Where's Kesteven Infirmary?'

'About an hour by car. Not too far.'

'I'll take you,' Joanna said, 'don't worry.'

The doctor continued, 'Meanwhile no school for a few days until we find out exactly what's wrong, just in case.'

Just in case what? Louisa May wondered. The doctor skimmed the notes the nurse had taken, then peered at Joanna. 'You were planning on returning to Manchester tonight?'

Joanna nodded, adding calmly, 'Yes, but it's out of the question now. I'll tell my boss I'm taking extra time off. I couldn't possibly leave my niece to face all this alone.'

'Is there not a Mr Haddock?'

'He's at sea,' Louisa May informed her.

'Ah, that's too bad. We think your mother will be in hospital for a while. Is there any way of contacting him?'

Before Louisa May could reply, Joanna interrupted. 'I'll deal with all that. Will we be able to visit tomorrow?'

'Tomorrow? Can't I see her now?' Louisa May asked, her voice trembling. 'I can say goodbye to her, can't I?'

The doctor frowned and then shrugged. 'I shouldn't let you really but if you've been sharing a room with your mother all this time I suppose five more minutes won't make much difference.'

* * *

Georgette moaned slightly as Louisa May kissed her cheek. 'Please get well, Mum, please.'

For the first time that day, Georgette responded. 'Louisa May.'

'I'm here.'

'Where will you be when they take me away?'

'With Joanna.'

'Oh. Tell her she's not to let them take you into care, Louisa May. Make her promise. They can be really persuasive these people, if you're not used to it.' Pain flitted cruelly across Georgette's tightly closed eyes.

'Don't talk if it hurts,' Louisa May whispered.

'Louisa May?'

'Yes?' She bent closer.

'Find her.'

'Find who?'

Georgette swallowed painfully, her throat parched and raw. 'Wendy Almond.'

'Why?'

'It's time.'

'Why now, though?'

'It's the right time.'

Louisa May stood up, confused by the demand. Then she remembered Georgette's pet phrase, that she didn't want to see Wendy Almond until she was dying, then she'd 'spit in her eye'. Urgently, Louisa May leaned across to reassure her mother. 'You're not dying. The doctor said you're not dying.'

But Georgette had shrunk away, drawing herself deeper into the bed like a sea-swept anemone.

Moments later the curtains were drawn back, and Staff Nurse Rook laid a sympathetic hand on the little girl's shoulder. 'We need to get Mum into the ambulance now,' she said.

Louisa May leaned across and kissed her mother's hair. 'Goodbye, Mama,' she whispered.

On the other side of the curtain, Joanna held out her hand. Louisa May took it, comforted by its protective grip. 'Everything OK?' Joanna asked.

Louisa May stared down at the grey tiled floor. 'I want to go back now,' she replied.

On returning to the hotel, they spent the first hour dragging furniture and bedding from one doorway to another as Joanna had decided it was best if they slept in her room.

Louisa May coped by pretending she knew exactly what Georgette was doing each minute. As she struggled with her mattress, her mother was arriving at Kesteven hospital. When she tucked her sheets into her bed on the floor, Georgette was being carried on a stretcher into one of the wards.

At suppertime, Louisa May managed to drink hot chocolate because she could picture a nurse helping Georgette take a sip of water. It was only when darkness fell and Louisa May realized she was about to spend the first night of her life away from her mother that she needed reassurance.

'My mum will be OK, won't she? By herself?'

Joanna, leaning down over the edge of her bed, nodded. 'Kesteven Infirmary has a good reputation. She'll be well looked after.'

'We can see her tomorrow, can't we?'

'If the doctors say so.'

'She's not dying.'

'No, she's not dying.'

'I told you it wasn't flu.'

'You did, smarty pants.' Joanna hesitated, but decided Louisa May needed to be prepared for the worst. 'Listen, we need to sort something out for when the Health Visitor comes.'

Louisa May thought for a moment. 'Yeah, you mean the bit about being Mum's twin sister, don't you? You should just have said sister.'

'That's not the bit I'm worried about, it's the rest of it, the holiday story—Lincoln and everything.'

'It's OK. Even if they find out you fibbed they won't tell you off or anything; you're a grown-up.'

'Lou, I shouldn't have lied . . . I've probably made things worse . . . they're going to start asking me questions about our medical history and if I make it up I could put your mum in danger.'

'It won't, Joanna, it won't.'

'Listen to me, Lou. There's more; when Social Services find out I'm not really your auntie I don't think they'll let you stay with me. They'll probably want to take you into care.'

Louisa May shuddered as if a gust of icy wind had blasted into her face. 'Care?'

'I'm guessing, but looking at it from their point of view, they can't leave a little girl alone in a hotel.'

'I don't want to go into care.'

'I don't want you to either but I'm not exactly Mary Poppins, am I?'

'I won't go! I'll run away.'

Joanna patted Louisa May's back. 'Are you sure you haven't got any real relatives? Anyone that would come and stay here with you until your mum was better?'

Louisa May kicked at her mattress, digging her toes into the orange cover time and time again.

'Daniel Brody might turn up.'

Joanna took a deep breath. 'Lou, there's as much chance of him turning up as there is of me winning the lottery; and I don't buy tickets.'

There was no point arguing, Louisa May decided. Nobody understood about Daniel Brody except her and Georgette, not even well-meaning people like Joanna. 'Well, there's always Wendy Almond, then,' Louisa May stated.

'The baby-in-the-dustbin woman. I thought neither of you wanted anything to do with her?'

Louisa May shrugged miserably. 'It doesn't matter if it means I can stay with you. Anyway, even Mum said it was time.'

Joanna reached down to pull the bed covers over her young guest's shoulders. 'Well, if your mum says it's time, then it's time. We'll start with the Salvation Army first thing tomorrow.'

'Why?'

'They're good at finding missing people. They have something called a Missing Person's Bureau.'

'But I know where she is. We've got letters.'

'Letters?'

'The ones I told you about, that kept arriving.'

Joanna slapped herself on the head, glad to be able to act the clown after the tension of the day. 'Of course! Ze letters! Zen ze case eez as good az cracked. Ze Wendy Almond will stay 'ere wiz 'er grand-daughter for a few wicks and buy 'er and 'er good friend Joanna plenty of sweeties, yes? And when ze mother, Mrs 'Addock is better, we vill all live 'appily ever after. What you say, Lou-Lou?'

Louisa May felt too drained to respond cheerfully. 'Goodnight, Joanna,' she replied softly, turning over to go to sleep. She pictured Georgette in her hospital bed, tucked in neatly, medicines by her side. Every now and again a nurse would go up to her and check she was all right, take her temperature, and walk away. 'That Mrs Haddock has made a remarkable recovery,' the nurse would inform the doctor.

Louisa May snuggled down. If it was any different, she would know. She would feel it.

Eleven

Before breakfast the next morning Joanna taught Louisa May how to use her mobile phone. 'You call the hospital while I go brush my teeth.'

Louisa May nervously dialled the hospital number. The busy receptionist on the switchboard couldn't tell her very much except that 'Mrs Haddock had spent a comfortable night in the Isolation Ward and was having tests carried out. No visitors would be allowed until further notice and then only close relatives.'

'That's me,' Louisa May declared as the line went dead.

The fox-fur glistened at her from the mantelpiece where it had been draped ready for what Joanna called 'the big moment'. Lifting the pelt down, Louisa May wound it round her neck, wondering what 'further notice' meant and wishing she had asked more questions.

When Joanna returned, bringing Mrs Bannister with her, Louisa May insisted on wearing the fur into breakfast.

Joanna nodded understandingly. 'Just don't let Ambrose nab it for the evening meal,' she warned.

Downstairs, Louisa May stirred her cornflakes round and round in their bowl, missing Georgette more in the dining room than anywhere else. She glanced across at the window table, which still had Stephen Deacon's breakfast things strewn across it.

'His lordship managed to drag himself out of bed, then,' Joanna said sarcastically, following Louisa May's gaze.

At that moment, Wanda, puffing nervously on a cigarette, flounced into the room. 'What's all this about 'ospitals? What's the matter with 'er?' she hissed in a low voice, even though there was nobody else to hear.

Joanna leaned back, her own voice booming. 'We don't know yet. Something to do with poor housing conditions.'

Wanda paled, as if this was the worst news possible.

'Well, whatever she's got, she didn't catch it 'ere. She's only been 'ere two minutes. She must 'ave brought it with 'er.'

Joanna laid a confiding hand on Wanda's arm. 'Of course she must. We'll all vouch for that, and when the Health Visitor comes—'

''Ealth Visitor?'

'And when the Health Visitor comes with the Sanitation Inspector and Chief Fire Officer, they'll have nothing but praise for your high standards, Wanda. You've nothing at all to worry about.'

'Inspector for . . . when? When're they coming?' Wanda's voice had almost disappeared.

Joanna shrugged. 'They didn't say. Could be tomorrow, could be next week.'

The agitated landlady pinched the end of her cigarette closed with her long nails and headed towards the kitchen.

'Ambrose! Ambrose!' she shrieked. 'We're being inspected. Get those mouse traps shifted.'

'What's bothering her?' Louisa May asked.

Joanna smiled knowingly. 'Having the hotel swarming with Health Visitors is the last thing the Putlocks want. They know Social Services will stop sending them clients if they see how they run this dump. Wanda might go on about us "spongers" but she needs us as much as we need her. Even the big hotels on the front struggle to survive now that everyone goes abroad for their holidays. Without us "social cases" filling her middle table, Wanda would be bankrupt.'

'What will happen?'

Joanna stretched an arm around Mrs Bannister's frail shoulders, drawing her close. 'We'll have warm rooms and decent meals for a while, won't we, Dorothy? So they can impress those nice Social Services people.'

An unimpressed Mrs Bannister brushed Joanna's hand away and grunted. Louisa May returned to her cornflakes, spooning the milk then letting it drip back into the bowl time and time again. She would rather have Georgette here than the best meals and the best rooms in all of England.

After breakfast, Louisa May sat with the flattened fox-fur across her knees, passing the letter from the solicitor in Leeds over to Joanna. The other letter, addressed simply to Georgette, weighed heavily in her hand.

'How many of these did you say you'd had?' Joanna asked, peering at the official notepaper.

Louisa May tried to remember. 'I don't know. Loads.'

'And when did you start getting them?'

'Ages ago. Over a year.'

'Well, here goes. If this turns out OK, you'll have a grandma to look after you until your mum recovers. Grandmas always spoil their grandkids to bits. It's an unwritten law.' She grinned reassuringly at Louisa May's unconvinced features and began to read.

Joanna's eyes narrowed more and more the further down the page she read. 'This Wendy Almond sounds desperate to get in touch: " . . . anxious to establish

communication with you in order to settle your estate.''
Settle your estate? Blinking heck, Lou, listen, you must
take whatever it is she's giving you. This is your
chance.'

'Chance?'

'Chance to get a life, a proper life.'

'We've got a proper life here. Well, when Mum comes
out of hospital we have.'

'Here?' Joanna stared at Louisa May in disbelief.

'What's wrong?'

'Lou, it sounds as if there's money just waiting for you
to collect it. This is your chance to find out there's more
to life than stainless steel teapots and burnt sausages.'

Louisa May shrugged. Stainless steel teapots and burnt
sausages were all she knew. Joanna leaned her head to
one side, her forehead creasing into a questioning frown.
'You do want to get out of this hole you're in, don't
you? I listened to what you told that nurse yesterday
about that room you used to sleep in in Lincoln. Your
mum wouldn't be in hospital now if you . . . well,
anyway . . . '

Shrugging away 'that room', Louisa May replied
calmly. 'We can't help it if we're ''have-nots''. It's not
our fault.'

'I know, but money from Wendy Almond can stop
you being a ''have-not'' as you call it.'

'But you've got money and you're still here.' It seemed
a fair enough point to make.

Joanna waved her arms around, trying to break
through what she saw as her young room-mate's
stubbornness. 'I'm only here because I'm stupid. I can
get out of here anytime I want to by phoning home on
that thing.' She pointed to the mobile on top of the
television set. 'The fact is, Lou, I lied to you.'

'What do you mean?' Louisa May asked. Joanna couldn't quite meet her eyes.

'I never got my degree. I couldn't take the pressure and ran away during the exams. When I eventually went home to tell Mum and Dad they'd already bought me the car and put a notice in the paper and everything. I couldn't bear to tell them the truth so I told them I'd got a job in France that started straight away. I phone home every Sunday telling them I'm in Calais.'

'So your mum's not in Australia?'

'No,' Joanna sniffed, 'she's in Cheadle.'

'Well, I'm still glad you came here instead.'

'It was the worst place I could find . . . I'm just a fraud, Lou. I've not been through anything like you and your mum and Mrs Bannister.'

'It doesn't matter.'

'It does!' Joanna began to cry.

'Do you want a muffin?' Louisa May asked, upset at how distraught Joanna was.

'No, I want you to open that ruddy letter!' Joanna retorted, trying to laugh.

'OK, if it'll make you happy.' Louisa May curled her toes and gazed at the sealed letter in her hand.

'Look, if you open the letter now, you'll know what's what, right? Then you can decide what we do next. If Wendy Almond sounds OK, you can go ahead. If she sounds as if she's off her rocker, we'll wait until your mum's well enough to sort it all out for herself. The letter does say "urgent" though. Time might be important.'

Louisa May stared at the envelope. Time. Georgette had said it was time. Joanna was right. Time was important. With clumsy, nervous fingers, she edged open the seal, sliding the letter out slowly like a celebrity about to announce a special prize.

'If there's a chain of biscuit shops involved, remember who your friends are,' Joanna instructed.

The letter was messily written, with crossings out on every page. It was hard to follow and didn't seem to make any sense. 'I don't understand it,' Louisa May said disappointedly, screwing her eyes up to decipher the small script.

'Why don't you read it out loud?' Joanna suggested.

'All right,' Louisa May agreed, trembling slightly. She began slowly, taking a sentence at a time, pausing in between. 'Dear Georgette Haddock, I have written and re-written this letter so many times . . . that in the end I have decided to just come right out with it as we do in Yorkshire . . . I suppose you must be wondering what on earth I'm up to getting in touch with you after all these years, especially as our Gary always did tell me it was none of my business—'

'"Our Gary"—that's very Yorkshire,' Joanna interrupted.

Louisa May continued. 'But I feel having a grandchild is my business . . . I know you felt very strongly about the baby being yours and only yours but all that was ten years ago and I hope you'll be kind enough to let me meet your daughter, my granddaughter, (we don't even know her name) now that our Gary's gone.

'I don't suppose our Gary's passing on means much to you (it's just over a year now) but surely you will allow his child some knowledge of him? Whether you like it or not she is our flesh and blood. I'm not the interfering sort, if that's what's worrying you. All I want is to see the girl and pass on to her what is hers by rights. She was his only offspring, when all's said and done, and my only grandchild, as far as I know. I do have to ask why you move around such a lot. If you don't mind me saying so, that much flitting can't be good for the child's education.

'Anyway, I hope this personal letter will convince you to get in touch . . .'

Louisa May stopped, her face bewildered. 'It's rubbish, isn't it? She doesn't even mention leaving Mum in the hospital, or why, or anything.'

Joanna, too, seemed bewildered. 'May I have a look?' she asked. Louisa May handed her the letter in silence and Joanna read and re-read it several times. 'Are you sure Georgette thinks Wendy Almond is her mother?' she said eventually.

'Of course she does. Why?'

The reply was delayed until Joanna double-checked the scrawled pages. 'I think Wendy Almond is your grandma.'

'I know that already.'

Joanna rubbed her forehead nervously. 'Lou, I think Wendy Almond is your grandma because "Our Gary" is your daddy.'

'Daniel Brody is my—'

Joanna shook her head, begging Louisa May with moist eyes. 'Forget all that red rose stuff, Lou, please. Come on, away at sea for ten years? He'd have webbed feet by now! Are you sure your mum's never mentioned a Gary before?'

'Never. She'd think Gary was a common name.'

Joanna skimmed through the letter again, frowning, leaving Louisa May shrinking inside. Opening that thing had been a big mistake, like peeking at a Christmas present early and finding a set of vests instead of anything decent. It had been one big waste of time.

Joanna fumbled for the mobile. 'Why don't I call these guys and let them sort it all out?' Carefully, she dialled the number, checking each digit she pressed with the one on the notepaper.

Louisa May stared stonily ahead, only breathing out when Joanna groaned into the receiver, 'Bummer! Answerphone!' and dropped the instrument on to the bed. 'I'll try again later.'

'I thought you said I could decide what we did?' Louisa May asked crossly.

'You can,' Joanna replied, 'but we've got to get somewhere first.'

'There's nowhere to get!' Louisa May stated, glaring at the blank television screen.

The day dragged between phone calls. First Joanna would try the solicitor's office, then Louisa May would try the hospital. Eventually, Joanna left her name and number on the tape machine while Louisa May despaired about being told the same message each time: 'Mrs Haddock is comfortable.'

When she went to bed that night it was much more difficult for Louisa May to imagine what Georgette would be doing. She seemed further away, harder for her thoughts to reach. But she is comfortable, Louisa May whispered to the fox-fur.

Twelve

A finger of bright sunshine filtered its way through the gap between the thin curtains, waking Louisa May early. She sat up, rubbing her eyes, forgetting at first where she was until Joanna's ear-shattering snores reminded her.

The memory of Joanna's confession made Louisa May feel stronger this morning. If even Joanna, with her car and money and cupboards full of ginger nuts, told lies and ran away, then the haves were not much different from the have-nots. No, Louisa May decided. She was not going to lie there waiting for things to happen. Waiting for strangers to turn up and put her into care, waiting for solicitors to call back about this Wendy Almond woman. Maybe she was only a kid, but kids could do things too.

Sliding from her bed, she found the telephone, and immediately dialled the hospital number, determined to ask questions this time. A voice answered cheerfully, 'Good morning, Kesteven Hospital?'

Louisa May gulped, fighting for the right words. She had been expecting the usual cold reply and the operator's friendly tone threw her off-track. 'Hell-o,' the voice sang.

'I want my mum,' Louisa May whispered, suddenly close to tears, despite herself.

'Aw. What ward is she on, ducky?'

'I . . .Isolation.'

'Give me her name, then, ducky; I'll find her for you. Are you missing her? You must be to call at six o'clock in the morning!'

Louisa May nodded into the phone. 'Her name's Mrs Haddock.'

'Mrs Haddock . . . Mrs Haddock . . . here we are, ducky, Georgette Haddock. It might be a bit tricky on that ward but I'll put you through to the desk. They'll tell you how she is. She's probably fast asleep though, ducky.'

'I just want to know if she's all right.'

''Course you do. It's only natural. I've eleven grandkids, I know how they miss their mum when she's in the maternity. Hang on, sweetheart.'

Louisa May waited, her heart pounding. At last she might find out something. There was a ringing, then a click, then a woman's weary voice. 'Staff Nurse Morris.'

'I'm . . . I'm Louisa May.'

The tired tone disappeared. 'Ah! I know all about you, Louisa May.'

'Do you?' she asked, surprised.

'I do! We were going to phone you later on this morning. We'd like you to come for a visit tomorrow.'

'Can I? To see my mum?'

'Yep. Ask for Dr Beecham first, though. He'll need to have a chat to you and your auntie. It's important.'

'OK.'

'Is your auntie there?'

'Auntie?'

'The one who's looking after you? Joanna, is it?'

A loud snore prompted Louisa May's brain. 'Oh, yes, she's asleep though.'

'So would I be, given half the chance. Will you remember to tell her about visiting the doctor? Save me a phone call? Or shall I call later?'

'No, I'll tell her, I promise.'

'Lovely, and I'll tell your mum I've spoken to you; she'll cheer up no end. See you tomorrow, then.'

'Yes. Tomorrow.'

'By the way?'

'Yes?'

'Is your mum's first name Georgette or Rosanna? She doesn't seem quite sure sometimes.'

'Oh,' Louisa May replied blithely, 'it varies!'

Humming to herself, Louisa May gave the mobile to one of the teddies to look after. She was ready to face the day.

Joanna, though, was not quite ready, at ten past six, to face anything. 'That's wonderful, Lou, but could you tell me again at eight o'clock? I was just about to marry Mel Gibson.' She yawned heavily and turned over, the mattress dipping into a giant grimace as its occupant went back to her dreams.

Wide-awake and excited, Louisa May dressed and slipped quietly back into her own room. First, she fastened the drooping curtain round the wire from which it dangled like damp washing. The sun raced through, wrapping her in golden warmth, lighting the room with its radiance.

Almost dancing, Louisa May began to tidy up. She dragged all Georgette's covers from the bed, shaking them one by one, getting rid of the coughs and the sweat and pain with each shake.

After that, Louisa May set all the books against the back of the dressing table, beginning with the first two stolen from Doncaster and finishing with the Lincoln edition of *The Trials of Rosanna Van Der Lees*. It was after they had moved from Doncaster the first Wendy Almond letter had arrived, she realized. Her eyes swept along the twenty-three volumes which awaited return to eleven different libraries. 'If you don't mind me saying so, you move around a lot,' that woman had written. Well, she did mind her saying so.

'I am not going to think about you today, Wendy Almond,' Louisa May said out loud, 'it's sunny and I'm happy.' She emptied the margarine tub of its 'complimentary' coffee sachets and tea bags then arranged them into a neat fan ready for when her mother came home.

The sunshine continued to pour into the room, making her restless. Closing the door behind her, she stole downstairs and into the raw brightness of the new day.

Being alone did not worry her, especially once she had reached the beach. She was free. Free to do anything. The tide was just going out, leaving heaps of newly dredged seaweed ribboning the water's edge. Louisa May poked at the deep, leafy tentacles with a stick, hoping to find treasure.

She picked her way towards the sheltering cliff-face, searching for shells and coloured stones on her way. Next to a cluster of large pebbles she found an empty burger box into which she dropped her salty bric-à-brac.

In the distance, the sea sparkled and she automatically thought of Daniel Brody. Her eyes scoured the grey North Sea for his ship but the horizon remained empty. In her head, a quiet voice whispered, 'told you so', but she pushed it away. Joanna did not know everything. Joanna made mistakes too.

Reaching for her carton, she chose a rounded piece from a broken bottle and began to rub off the sand, polishing the glass until it shone like a precious green stone. Absorbed, she buffed and polished the rest of her treasures, surprised by how beautiful they were. She would take them to the hospital tomorrow and give them to Georgette as a present. Squashing down the carton lid, she walked slowly back to the hotel.

Joanna hardly took any notice of Louisa May's beach collection. 'I nearly had a fit when I couldn't find you. Fancy going out on your own! What if some weirdo had got you?'

'I thought all the weirdos lived in the hotel, not outside it,' Louisa May joked.

'Hmm! There's a certain logic to that statement, I suppose,' Joanna mumbled, unconvinced, before going to fetch Mrs Bannister.

But once inside the dining room, Louisa May's unsanctioned walk was forgotten. Joanna grabbed her arm and smiled. 'What did I tell you?' she cried.

On the sideboard—on the freshly polished, overflowing-ashtray-free sideboard—were two glass bowls full of cereal with a jug of fresh milk next to them. 'Oh,' said Louisa May, 'it's help-yourself!'

A disgruntled Ambrose stood waiting for them at the table. 'English or Continental?' he muttered.

'Pardon me?' Joanna teased.

'You heard,' Ambrose replied gruffly.

'We'll stay traditional, I think. We've got a busy day ahead of us. Thank you, landlord,' Joanna replied, confidently answering for all of them.

'What busy day?' Louisa May asked.

Joanna winked. 'You'll see.'

Cereal was enough for Louisa May, especially when she saw the plateful of food Wanda had sniffily given to Joanna. Sausages, properly cooked, bacon, tomatoes, and triangles of fried bread encircling a mound of scrambled egg. 'Just as good as you'd get anywhere on the front,' Wanda declared. 'Prob'ly better. Make sure you tell anyone 'oo visits that, an' all.'

'I'm sure you're right,' Joanna agreed. 'By the way, Wanda?' she said sweetly.

'What?'

'There's something wrong with the radiators in our rooms.'

'Wrong?'

'Yeah, I'm not sure what it is. They're leaking this stuff; it's all warm and seems to be filling the room. I think it's called heat.'

Wanda swore under her breath. 'You want to get back in the knife drawer with all the other sharp things,' she retorted.

The landlady was about to leave when she dug into her skirt pocket and brought out a white envelope which she patted next to Louisa May's cereal bowl. 'That's for your mam from Mr Deacon, though I did point out to 'im I am not 'is go-between.' With that, she tottered back into the kitchen.

Louisa May stared suspiciously at the envelope. She'd had enough of these things lately. The name Rosanna, illuminated with tiny roses, almost filled the front.

'Oh, how cute,' Joanna mocked. 'Are you going to open it?'

'No. I'll give it to Mum tomorrow,' Louisa May replied firmly, tucking the envelope into her jeans. She wasn't falling for that one again.

'Right, tomorrow. Tell me again what the nurse said about me.'

'She just asked if my auntie was there.'

'Right,' Joanna repeated, dipping the tip of her sausage into her egg, 'there's a chance we might get away with it, matey. If they still think I'm your auntie they won't have got in touch with Social Services yet, and even if they do, by the time they get their finger out—'

'We don't need to bother with those solicitor people in Leeds, either, do we?' Louisa May interrupted.

Joanna chewed, waving her fork from side to side. 'Well, that's a different ball game.' She reached across for the brown sauce. 'Why?'

'Nothing,' Louisa May lied.

'It'll turn out OK. I can feel it in my bones.'

Louisa May watched as Joanna began on her second rasher of bacon. 'What else can you feel in your bones?'

'Love,' she replied instantly.

'Love?' It was a strange answer, Louisa May thought.

Joanna nodded. 'I can feel the love between you and your mum which is so strong that nothing could ever destroy it.'

Louisa May smiled with pleasure, her cheeks burning as if the sun had followed her into the dining room.

Joanna continued, her voice more serious. 'And I can feel Wendy Almond's love for a grandchild she's never seen but feels so much for.'

This time, Louisa May shuffled uncomfortably in her seat. Her stomach churned. 'I don't want to think about her. She's stupid.'

'She keeps popping up though, doesn't she? Barging into your head when you least expect it? Nagging you like an invisible toothache? My parents do that all the time and Cheadle's further away than Leeds!'

'My Emerald barges in,' Mrs Bannister said unexpectedly, her chin coated in egg yolk.

Joanna leaned across and wiped the yolk away with a tissue. 'See! Even Emerald barges in, whoever or whatever Emerald is!'

Louisa May laughed too loudly at Mrs Bannister's comment. Relieved at the diversion, she fished into her back pocket for one of the pieces of green glass she had found. 'Look, Mrs Bannister,' she said eagerly, 'an emerald!'

Mrs Bannister stared at the polished object for a long time. When she spoke, her chin wobbled, as if she was about to cry, but her voice was startlingly clear. 'Emerald's eyes were deeper than that, flecked with gold. Irish eyes, Daddy said.'

'Who was Emerald?' Joanna asked gently.

'My sister, you fool, who do you think?' the old woman retorted angrily. Without warning she reached across and snatched the glass from Louisa May's hand, swiftly dropping it down the front of her blouse.

'Good job her sister didn't have eyes like a jellyfish, then!' Louisa May giggled.

Joanna grinned. 'Another problem solved. Ve are doing vell!'

'I couldn't look after her like you do,' Louisa May said.

''Course you could, if you were older. You just have to be patient, that's all. And speaking of patients, we've got some shopping to do before we see your mum tomorrow.'

'What sort of shopping?'

'You know—this and that.'

Louisa May wagged her finger at 'Auntie' Joanna. 'You don't need any more biscuits.'

'Who mentioned biscuits?' Joanna replied innocently, wobbling her eyebrows like drunken caterpillars.

Thirteen

The automatic doors of the main hospital entrance slid smoothly open in front of Joanna and Louisa May, wafting them with warm air. Inside the lobby, they were overwhelmed with shops and cafés and towering rubber plants.

'Wow! I wouldn't mind coming here for my holidays,' Joanna said, leading the way to the reception desk. As she left to speak to a man with a bald head, Louisa May slid the fox-fur from round her over-hot neck and dangled it across her free arm.

In her other hand, she clutched a bagful of gifts bought during yesterday's shopping spree. Excitement bubbled up in her stomach at the thought of seeing Georgette's face when she gave her all these things.

Joanna had paid for everything, looking hurt when Louisa May had fussed about the cost. What sort of an auntie did she want people to think she was she had argued. Mean and nasty? Louisa May had told her nobody could ever call her that. Hopping from one foot to the other, Louisa May waited impatiently for her 'auntie' to finish talking.

At last, Joanna thanked the bald man and pointed towards a corridor. 'This is where we have to tread carefully, Lou. If we can bluff our way with this lot, we might stand a chance if Social Services turn up,' she instructed.

'I know.' Louisa May smiled. It was hard remembering to be serious. All she wanted was to see Georgette.

At the entrance to the Isolation Ward Joanna introduced herself to the nurse sitting at the desk, who traced a finger down the roster on which she was doodling.

Louisa May listened closely, wondering if it was the same nurse she had spoken to on the phone, the one who 'knew all about her', but this one had a high-pitched, annoying voice. It was definitely not her.

'You've had clearance to see Mrs Haddock? This is Isolation, you know. We get some very contagious diseases,' the nurse squeaked.

Joanna put her head to one side. 'We were specifically invited by Staff Nurse Morris.'

The nurse checked her list again. 'It says here that the little girl can visit but you need to see Dr Beecham first. He's due in half an hour when he's finished his rounds.'

'Why is it all right for one and not the other? Mrs Haddock is my sister!'

'I'm sure she is but we've had medical information about the little girl, Louisa May, but not you. You must see Dr Beecham.'

Joanna glanced at her watch. 'OK, if I must, I must.' She turned to Louisa May. 'You go see your mum and I'll grab a coffee.' Their eyes held for a second. 'Go steady,' she added.

Georgette's small room was immediately next to the reception area. She was propped up against a mountain of pillows, her freshly washed hair spilling neatly round her pale face so that she looked like a wax doll in a gift box.

'Mum, Mum!' Louisa May flung herself on top of the bed, burying her head into her mother's neck.

'Louisa May,' Georgette whispered hoarsely. She let out a low cry which told Louisa May just how much she had been missed.

'Are you better? Has the cough gone?' Louisa May gabbled.

Georgette smiled and nodded, trying to cover up her emotions. 'Nearly. Isn't it wonderful? Tuberculosis!'

'Tuberculosis? What's that?'

Georgette stroked her daughter's head, continuing dreamily, 'Only the most romantic illness of them all!'

'Romantic?'

'All the best Victorians had TB, especially writers and poets, except it was usually called consumption then. Rosanna had it in chapter fifteen of *The Trials*,' Mrs Haddock explained, gazing fondly at her daughter through blood-shot eyes.

'Will I get it?'

'No. They innoculated you soon after you were born. They said you were a "high-risk" baby,' Georgette glowered, offended at the memory.

Louisa May changed the subject quickly, wanting to keep the visit light-hearted and happy. 'Oh. Is that all your medicine?' she asked, turning to a mass of brown plastic bottles huddled on top of an otherwise empty cabinet.

Georgette nodded. 'I rattle like a tube of Smarties when I walk!'

Giving her mother another cuddle, Louisa May told her it did not matter what she sounded like as long as she got better. Her eyes stung as she spoke. It felt so good to be near her again.

Bending down, she reached for the carrier bag. 'I've brought you all these,' she said, hauling the gifts on to the bed. Georgette smiled broadly through dry lips as

one present after another was revealed. 'Chocolates,'
Louisa May announced, sliding the box on to the
cabinet. 'Fruit . . . blackberry mineral water . . . lemon
squash and . . . a sloppy book. Joanna chose that. I
chose everything else.'

'How lovely!' Georgette cried, running a finger over
the embossed cover of the paperback.

Louisa May arranged the bottles and fruit behind
the medicine. 'You're like any ordinary patient now,'
she boasted, wishing her mother could be on a shared
ward so she could compare her cabinet with the
others.

Her mother plucked at her white sheet. 'I've missed
you so much, Louisa May. It's been awful for me in here
knowing you're all alone in that place. I didn't know
what was happening. I daren't say anything in case . . .
you know . . . they took you away. I was so worried.'

Louisa May was quick to reassure her. 'Oh, I'm fine.
Joanna's really great and Wanda's put the heating on
and there's nice food and Mrs Bannister said something
normal for once—'

'Oh. You seem to be getting on just fine without me,
then.' The words were tinged with disappointment.

Sensing she had made a mistake, Louisa May leaned
across to comfort her. 'No way! It's not the same without
you at all. I have to pretend I know exactly what you're
doing so I can even get to sleep.'

Georgette plucked even harder at the sheet. 'Me too.
It's been the worst time of my life.'

Louisa May tightened her hug but her mother let out
a gasp of pain. 'It still hurts a little, if you press on too
much,' she said, protecting her chest.

'But you are getting better? The cough will go, won't
it? Then you can come back to the hotel?'

'Yes. I'm getting better. I'll be out in a couple of weeks I think.'

'Brilliant!'

Georgette examined her nails. 'I suppose I'm the talk of Cliff Top. Has . . . has Mr Deacon said anything?'

'Oh, yes. He's sent a letter. It's in Foxy.'

Her mother brightened, returning to her 'Rosanna' voice. 'It was so brave of him to whisk me downstairs in his strong arms,' she said softly.

'That wasn't—' Louisa May began but then she stopped. There was no point spoiling people's dreams. 'That wasn't a problem. He must be used to carrying things, with all those shoe boxes. Look, I found these on the beach for you.' From the bottom of the carrier, Louisa May produced the burger carton containing all her favourite shells and stones.

Georgette's eyes shone. 'Oh, Louisa May, pearls and opals from the sea! Now these are wonderful.' She held each object to the light in turn, clearly pleased.

Louisa May hesitated, wondering whether now would be a good time to mention Wendy Almond's letter but Joanna arrived, peering tentatively round the door, and the moment was lost. A tense smile was directed at both of them. 'Hi, Lou. Hello, Mrs Haddock. I managed to sneak in without anyone seeing me—some emergency's sent everyone scurrying off to another ward. How's it going?'

Georgette threw on her 'Rosanna' face. 'Superbly, thank you.'

'You look miles better than you did.'

'Thank you and . . .' Georgette paused, then lapsed into her everyday voice, 'thanks for everything you're doing. I really appreciate it, especially as you hardly know us.'

Joanna shrugged away the gratitude. 'It's nothing. I enjoy having the company, even if the company has nabbed all my ginger nuts!' She bit her lip. 'We've got to see Dr Beecham now. I hope he doesn't ask too much about our "shared" childhood or anything. I never had a sister, let alone a twin.'

Georgette pushed herself upright. 'I don't suppose I'd be in here if we had been twins,' she said wistfully.

'No, you'd be too busy eating walnut muffins!' Louisa May grinned, jumping down from the bed. She slipped the fox-fur round Georgette's neck. 'Mr Deacon's letter's in there; you can drool over that until we come back,' she teased.

Dr Beecham was a tall man with a bristly chin. As he ushered them into a side room, Joanna, deciding attack was the best form of defence, bombarded him with questions. 'Did you find out what's wrong with my sister? How long will she be in for? Is there anything I can do?'

Dr Beecham reached in his pocket for his glasses and indicated that Joanna should take a seat. 'Yes, indeed. Erm . . . firstly, you should know that Mrs Haddock has tuberculosis.'

Joanna gasped, setting Louisa May on edge. What was the matter? Georgette had been pleased. The doctor held up his hand, as if to stop traffic.

'It's all right. All her results indicate we caught it very early on.'

'But TB! I thought that had died out years ago.'

'The Victorians had it,' Louisa May said knowledgeably.

Dr Beecham smiled at her. 'They certainly did. Even after the war it was common until everyone had injections. I'm afraid it's on the increase again now, in certain . . . conditions.' His eyes probed Louisa May's sympathetically and she knew instantly what he meant. Homeless conditions. Poor conditions. High-risk baby conditions. She thought of Georgette's boiling hot body struggling to get through the night. It was not fair. Why were they always the ones with 'certain conditions'?

'May I?' The doctor held up a flat piece of wood the size of a teaspoon. 'I just need to look in your throat, to check you're all right.'

Reluctantly she stuck her tongue out. She had not bargained for any of this. He moved his head one way, then another. His hands smelt of pears. 'Good, good, that looks clear.' A cold stethoscope was pressed against her chest, with more murmurs of 'Good, good.'

Eventually, he patted Louisa May on the head. 'Just one last little thing for now; the Heaf test. Luckily we have managed to get hold of your medical records from Lincoln so I'm fairly confident about your immunity but . . . '

Opening the cabinet door above the sink, the doctor began taking out slim packages with the word 'sterile' printed across the front. Joanna wrinkled her nose at Louisa May, trying to be funny. 'The Heaf test. I know one—Hampstead Heaf. Who said a Geography degree wouldn't come in useful?'

'If you could roll up your sleeve,' Dr Beecham requested.

Louisa May obeyed, shaking inside, as he rubbed a cold cotton wool swatch against her wrist, talking calmly to her all the time.

'Although this has six needles, it won't hurt.'
'Six!'

'Six of the best! Mind you, according to your mother, injections haven't been invented yet!'

'She always did have a terrible memory,' Joanna explained, going pale at the sight of Louisa May's injection, which actually only stung slightly.

'Yes,' Dr Beecham agreed, a puzzled look on his face, 'she does seem a bit confused. Calls herself Mrs Haddock one minute and Van Der Lees the next.'

'Van Der Lees was her maiden name.'

'But yours is Frankish?'

'After my first husband! Frank Frankish,' Joanna lied quickly.

The doctor prepared a second syringe.

'Do I have to have another one?' Louisa May complained.

'No, this is for your auntie.'

'Me?'

'And everyone who's been in contact with Mrs Haddock recently. Our Health Visitor will be calling at your hotel very soon,' Dr Beecham informed them.

Louisa May's stomach lurched. 'I won't be taken into care, will I?' she blurted out.

Joanna was too engrossed in her six needles to shoot her a warning look.

He smiled briefly. 'No, not if you're being properly looked after by Auntie Squeamish here. Why, do you want to be taken into care?'

'No way!' Louisa May's legs felt weak and useless.

'Hey, it's not that bad, you know. My wife and I take in foster kids. We only ever eat the really naughty ones. Now, do you want me to explain to you about TB?' he asked quietly.

Louisa May stared at the injection mark. 'No,' she said, 'I already know enough.'

The doctor laid his hand gently on her shoulder. 'We're going to make your mummy better with lots of tablets and plenty of food. And when she leaves hospital you have to make sure she comes back here for her check-ups. Promise? It's the check-ups which are the most important.'

Louisa May nodded solemnly, used to being given responsibility for Georgette's appointments.

'Would you mind if I had a word with your auntie?' Dr Beecham asked.

'Fine,' she said, exchanging a hurried glance with Joanna. 'I'll be with Mum.'

Fourteen

Georgette had her back turned to the wall. For a moment, Louisa May thought she might be sleeping and walked stealthily round to the far side of the bed.

There she saw her mother was gazing blankly at the fox-fur. It had been stuffed into the shelf of the bedside cabinet, with sheets of paper fanning out beneath its lop-sided head. Moving closer, Louisa May recognized the messy writing on the pages.

'The doctor's talking to Joanna about something,' she began, then swallowed before adding lightly, 'You read Wendy Almond's letter, then? I forgot I'd put it back in the fox.' She hadn't forgotten at all. She had wrapped it round Stephen's envelope, knowing Georgette would see it.

Georgette's body sagged as she mumbled something into her pillow. Louisa May crouched over her. 'Pardon?'

Twisting round, her face as white as the sheets behind it, Georgette repeated her words. 'He was a plumber,' she said limply.

Louisa May trembled. She felt slightly giddy, as if she already knew everything she was about to hear. 'Who?' she asked anyway, her voice coming from far away.

Her mother seemed to be having the same experience, chopping out her words like a bad actress who knew her lines but was no good at delivering them. 'Gary Pritchard. He was a plumber who came to the home to fix the airing cupboard and mend the boilers.'

'So?'

Georgette sighed heavily, glancing round to check she was not being overheard. 'Gary Pritchard is your father. I didn't know him for very long; definitely not long enough for all this,' she grumbled, glancing quickly at the letter.

Louisa May couldn't look at her mother. She stared again at the tiny pink circle of dots on her wrist. Stared so hard they seemed to merge into one fleshy lump.

'And Daniel Brody wasn't real at all, was he?' she whispered.

In reply, Georgette wiped her damp eyes with the corner of her sheet. Louisa May edged her way on to her mother's bed, sliding her arm round the back of her shoulders the way she had seen Joanna do to Mrs Bannister. It always seemed to be such a comforting gesture.

'It's all right,' Louisa May said, surprised at how calm she felt. Deep down, she had known Daniel Brody was made up, even before Joanna had implied it; known but not wanted to believe. She had to hear it from her mother.

So, her father did not sail the ocean waves, his arms bronzed from his journeys between foreign lands, his heart aching for his little miracle at home in England. Her father was called Gary Pritchard. He was a plumber and he was dead. Now she knew. A sadness settled inside her, the sadness of a lost dream, but there was a new feeling, too. One she could not quite work out because she had never had it before. Whatever it was warmed her, sending tingling messages throughout her body.

'Do you hate me?' Georgette asked huskily, her head bowed to hide her tears which slid quietly down her face.

For a second, Louisa May, lost in her thoughts, did not reply, then she saw the tears and focused on the question.

'No! 'Course I don't hate you! Why should I?' Louisa May cried, shocked at the idea. 'You're my mum. You can't hate your mum. I understand.'

Georgette's shoulders suddenly collapsed sending Louisa May rolling off the bed and crashing to the floor at the unexpected movement. Momentarily, she thought she would cry but the sight of Georgette's anxious face peering down at her through a pair of round, red-rimmed eyes made her laugh out loud instead.

Scrambling to her feet, she rubbed her bruised bottom, still laughing. The anxiety on Georgette's face gradually disappeared until she, too, joined in.

Her rasping howls filled the room. 'Ooh! Ooh! It hurts, Louisa May, it hurts!'

'Your face!' Louisa May hooted, holding her aching ribs now. 'Why are your eyes all horrible anyway?'

'It's . . . these . . . tablets. You should see . . . my wee . . . it's orange!'

'Like Tango?'

Georgette dabbed at her eyes and her nose in between peals of laughter. 'Tell me I haven't, Louisa May!'

'Haven't what?'

Shaking her head from side to side, Georgette tried to calm down and gulped, 'Tell me I haven't spent my life running away from a mother-in-law!'

Yanking the letter from under the fox-fur, Georgette squinted at the writing in astonishment. 'What's she called Almond for anyway when he was called Pritchard?' she demanded. 'And why does she make me out to be some . . . some cold-hearted schemer? And as for all this "what's rightfully yours" business. Phh! He never had two pennies to rub together when I knew him. Spent everything on his precious motor bike.'

'Maybe he won the lottery,' Louisa May suggested.

'Maybe,' Georgette said, doubtfully, frowning again and again at the scrawl. She sniffed repeatedly like a piglet searching out food. The sound made Louisa May want to laugh again but a stillness had crept over Georgette, stiffening her face. 'So she didn't want to find me after all,' she said softly.

'Who?' Louisa May asked.

'My mother . . . my real mother. She didn't want to find me after all. What a waste! What a stupid, silly waste of . . . life! I'd forgiven her, too.'

Louisa May hesitated. 'Is that why you said it was time? When you first came into hospital?' she asked.

'Yes. I . . . Oh, I don't believe this!'

Groaning, Georgette fell back into her pillows, staring at the ceiling. 'What a waste! How ridiculous! Can you believe it?' With the mutterings came an anger, rising and rising through her scarred lungs. 'That's it!' she finally exclaimed.

'What is?' Louisa May questioned, half-wary, half-impressed by her mother's determined tone. It was the same tone she had used when she had telephoned the hospital yesterday morning. A don't-mess-with-me tone new to both of them.

'If she's not going to look for me, I'm going to look for her. I want answers!' Georgette grimly informed her daughter.

'We can go to the Salvation Army, they're good at finding people. Joanna told me,' Louisa May said.

Georgette nodded, then propped herself up to face Louisa May. 'I need to find her, Louisa May. I need to know why she left me in that hospital. She doesn't even have to see me; she can write the reason on the back of an old note to the milkman for all I care, but it's like Wendy Almond says, she is flesh and blood. Once I know why, I can . . . I can live. We can live. Can you understand that?'

The tingling sensation Louisa May had felt earlier fused into thousands of cold prickles shooting up and down her arms and legs. She understood. She understood that Wendy Almond's letter had changed their lives forever. It had given her much more than the promise of money, or whatever her inheritance was. It had given Louisa May a past and Georgette a future. They weren't have-nots any more.

'I love moments like that,' Joanna said as she drove out of Kesteven town centre, listening thoughtfully to Louisa May, whose face glowed as she told her story. 'It's called a revelation. That moment when a truth smashes you right between the eyes and you think, "Great big hairy bums! That explains everything!" There's a whole book of them in the Bible.'

'Hairy bums?' Louisa May asked.

'Yeah,' Joanna replied, grinning. 'Maybe that's where the Moonies came from.'

Louisa May groaned. 'Your jokes stink!'

'Thanks. And thanks for dropping me in it with Dr Lemsip.'

'Beecham.'

'Whatever. Anyway, he asked me why you were so worried you'd be fostered, thank you very much . . . '

'So-rree.'

'I told him you were highly strung.'

'Thanks back.'

'Seriously, though, I had to tell him the truth, Lou. I was scared he'd give Georgette the wrong medicine or something if I made up her medical history . . . but listen, don't panic. He started going on about how with the Children Act, Social Services put kids first whenever they can and try to find places where they'd feel most at home with carers that match up to their backgrounds.'

'So he only looks after other doctors' kids?'

'Something like that.'

Louisa May suddenly realized what Joanna was leading up to. 'Oh! So I'd be found a place in a hotel.'

Joanna nodded. 'Maybe.'

A wide smile broke across Louisa May's face. 'They'd never find anyone to match my mum. She's unique.'

'I know,' Joanna agreed, 'but there are plenty of us in similar circumstances, if not time-zones.'

'What, you mean . . . ?'

'I mean that, amazingly enough, single plump coconut-heads stand as much chance of fostering as posh married housewives.'

'What, and you'd foster me?'

'Sure. I could do with a slave.'

Louisa May stamped her feet up and down the crisp-packeted floor in excitement. 'Everything's turning out brilliantly,' she cried. 'Mum's nearly better, I can stay with you and, look, I even got my shoe money back from Stephen Deacon.' She yanked at the three ten pound notes thrust deep into her pockets which Georgette had folded into her hand as she was saying goodbye.

'No message from him,' Georgette had sniffed disappointedly.

Joanna grunted. 'Sneaky Deaky returning money? Revelations and miracles on the same day! You watch,

107

Wanda and Ambrose'll have turned into human beings when we get back.'

The driver and her passenger exchanged looks.

'Nahh!' they chorused.

During the evening meal, Louisa May's mood changed. Her mind buzzed, not with quick, clever ideas, but with frenzied, jangling thoughts. As one notion came into her head, another thrust its way on top of it, like an impatient man switching channels on his TV set.

Her lamb chop hardened on her plate as she tried to connect names with the things she was supposed to do with the names. Georgette had told her to thank Stephen Deacon for the money but Stephen Deacon wasn't there. And what was she supposed to do about Wendy Almond? And Gary Pritchard? She knew what sailors looked like, but not plumbers. How tall had he been? What did he talk like? How had he died?

Then there were other matters to think about, like the giro that was due again soon. Did she have to cash it or would Wanda try to pinch it again? And the Health Visitor business. Joanna had only said they might let her stay with her. Might. It seemed a long time since her peaceful walk along the beach.

After dinner, Joanna, who had seen the haunted look return to Louisa May's eyes, thrust a pen and notepad in the girl's direction. 'Write a Worries List,' she ordered.

'What's that?'

'It's like when you go shopping, only instead of crossing each thing off as you buy it, you cross each worry off as it goes away. It helps to get things into perspective. I wrote one in the hospital café.'

Louisa May chewed the end of the pen. 'Do I have to show it to you?' she asked.

'No,' Joanna said, feeding fifty p's into the meter, 'no point. I'm one of those new breed of failed graduates— can't read!' Grinning, she left the room to check on Mrs Bannister, stopping to poke her head round the door. 'I was kidding about not being able to read,' she added, 'I got as far as *Jennifer Yellow Hat.*'

There was no reply. Louisa May had begun her list.

Fifteen

Two mornings later, Louisa May waited anxiously for the arrival of her first worry on the list—Mrs Chambers from Social Services.

Joanna had telephoned Mrs Chambers to tell her what was happening, although she forgot to mention how Mrs Haddock had, until recently, been her twin sister. She talked until the batteries had run flat on her mobile, finally arranging the morning's meeting.

It was a meeting Louisa May was desperate to get over and done with. Once she knew she was safe, that she would be allowed to stay in the hotel with Joanna, she knew she would be able to concentrate on everything else.

Every time the dining room door opened she swivelled round. Joanna shook her head and nudged Mrs Bannister.

'Lou can't keep still today. Do you reckon she's got worms, Mrs B.?'

If Mrs Bannister had planned a reply it was interrupted by the doorbell ringing and the sound of voices. Louisa May pushed her cereal bowl away and looked to Joanna for guidance. The plan was to act cool. Joanna held two triangles of toast up to her eyes, making wholemeal sunglasses. 'Remember, normality at all times, Lou!'

Wanda and Ambrose bustled in first, followed closely by two women. Louisa May recognized Mrs Chambers, the lady who had given her chocolate marshmallows, straight away. Short and solid in black patent shoes, the head of Wathsea Social Services had an air about her which was both friendly and resolute. She smiled warmly at Louisa May, putting her at ease. Anyone this nice wouldn't send children into foster homes if they didn't want to go, would they?

A well-rehearsed Ambrose marched straight to the damp patch by the bay window, his burly arms folded like hairy harvest loaves across his chest. Wanda, pulling at the hemline of her miniskirt, began gushing about the hotel's finer features.

'And this is the dinin' room where our residents can participate in the best cuisine in the 'ole of Wathsea.'

The visitors exchanged knowing glances. Mrs Chambers laid her briefcase on the table. 'Sorry to arrive during breakfast, Mr and Mrs Putlock. This is Miss Ball, the Area Health Visitor. Is there anywhere she can give you your shots while I talk to Louisa May?'

Wanda blinked. 'Shots?'

'It's only six needles,' Louisa May added helpfully.

Miss Ball went on to explain. 'Just a precaution. All those who've been in contact with Mrs Haddock need to be tested for immunity against the TB.' She glanced round. 'You've had your injection, Miss Frankish?'

Joanna nodded. 'And Louisa May's had hers. The doctor is pretty sure the results will be negative.' Mrs Chambers looked at Joanna keenly, like a cautious shopper about to make a purchase, but she did not say anything.

Wanda pounced. 'What TB? Nobody said nothing to me about no TB. I'm not 'aving nobody in my hotel with TB.' She stared witheringly at Louisa May who felt her insides crumble. It had not occurred to her that Wanda might object. They were up-to-date with their rent. What more could she want?

Miss Ball was quick to reassure the landlady. 'It's all right, Mrs Putlock, Mrs Haddock's case is not a serious one. It's as well to have jabs anyway, in your line of business.'

'My line of business 'as nothing to do with TB,' Wanda pouted.

The Health Visitor glanced round the dining room. 'It's lovely and warm in here. Mrs Haddock'll recover in no time as long as the heating is maintained at this level.' She beamed at Ambrose. 'Miss Frankish told us about your quick thinking, Mr Putlock, in helping Mrs Haddock to the hospital. If only more hotel owners were as caring as you two, my life would be a lot easier.'

'He was a hero,' Joanna informed them, chancing a quick wink at Louisa May.

Ambrose scratched the burn mark on his arm. 'It was nothin',' he said gruffly.

Wanda interrupted. If there were any compliments going, she was having them, not that lump of lard in the corner. 'We like to think our residents look upon us as their friends. They've 'ad it rough, some of them. We like to do all we can to 'elp.' No one bothered to contradict her.

A medical kit was laid out on the sideboard. Louisa May recognized the sterilized needles inside. 'Is it ladies or gentlemen first?' Miss Ball asked. The landlord flinched.

Mrs Chambers slid a blue folder from her briefcase, and turned to Louisa May. 'Shall we go to your room and let them get on with it?' she asked.

Louisa May and Joanna rose together, leaving Ambrose protesting that 'nobody was sticking nothing in him'.

A dank fug hung over room five as they entered, the rising damp having taken tenancy now that no one lived there. Mrs Chambers glanced round briefly, and shook her head. 'We have a problem,' she said at last.

'I don't want to go into care,' Louisa May cried out. 'I want to stay here with Joanna. She's good at looking after people. She's got biscuits and a telly and a car.'

The Social Worker laughed. 'Biscuits, a telly, and a car! Everything a body needs! No, our problem is that we can't put you into care, love.'

'Can't?'

'Not in Wathsea. We don't have many foster places, and those we do have are full. In a nutshell, we don't know what to do with you.'

'So I can stay here?'

Mrs Chambers leaned against the radiator and turned to Joanna, casting her measuring eyes over her. 'Without beating about the bush, Miss Frankish, would you be willing to become a temporary foster carer for Louisa May until Mrs Haddock comes out of hospital?'

Joanna dug her hands into her pockets, pretending to give the question a lot of thought. After a while she shrugged. 'Why not?'

'You'd have to answer some questions of course, fill in some personal details.'

'Naturally.'

'And Louisa May does seem quite fond of you.'

'I'm going to be her slave,' Louisa May grinned.

'And you will be paid,' Mrs Chambers added.

Joanna's steady gaze fell on to the bulging folder. 'And it will help you out of a tight spot, Mrs Chambers,' she said pointedly.

Mrs Chambers paused for a moment, then replied evenly, 'Yes, I admit it would. It's almost impossible finding accommodation for people like Mrs Haddock at short notice as it is, then when something goes wrong . . . '

An ominous crimson patch crept along Joanna's neck. 'Like when they're careless enough to catch TB because of being dumped in places like this by people like you!' she accused.

Mrs Chambers looked sternly at Joanna, radiating waves of panic through Louisa May. Why couldn't grown-ups get it right? Georgette never said anything to people in charge and Joanna said too much. Fortunately, Mrs Chambers didn't seem ruffled. Maybe she was used to being criticized. 'Mrs Haddock was lucky to have been given bed and breakfast at all. Many resorts are refusing to take people in from us now,' she replied calmly.

Joanna exploded. 'Lucky! If this is your idea of good luck I'd hate to see what you thought bad luck was!'

Mrs Chambers eyed the room again, sharing the young woman's anger but knowing there was nothing she could do about it. Her casebook was overflowing with applications from homeless families swept to her by colleagues in cities and towns. Mrs Haddock's case was not unusual, nor, worryingly, was she her only client with TB.

'Joanna, are you willing to look after the little girl or not? There's a children's home in—'

Joanna reached over to Louisa May, holding her close. 'Of course I'm willing to look after her. I just didn't think it would be this easy.'

'You'll be properly vetted,' Mrs Chambers snapped, signalling she'd had enough criticism for one morning.

Joanna suddenly laughed, a raucous laugh that could have cracked plaster. 'Does that mean if I roll over I get my tummy tickled?' she joked. 'And free doggy-chocs?'

114

'She eats anything, Mrs Chambers,' Louisa May informed her proudly.

After Mrs Chambers had gone downstairs, Louisa May gave Joanna a grateful hug, her thin arms stretching to reach round her guardian's plump middle. 'That's one off your list, pumpkin,' Joanna said.

'Yes,' Louisa May agreed, 'only four hundred and six to go!'

'What number was starting school?'

'It wasn't. You said a list of worries, not tortures!'

Joanna unclasped herself. 'Well, school's on my list. I'm going to check with that Miss Bat—'

'Ball! Stop being annoying!'

'—to see when you can start. Education's very important.'

'You sound like my mum.'

'Well, I'm supposed to. This is a serious commitment for me, Louisa May Haddock. I may even buy name-tapes.'

She glided importantly out, leaving Louisa May to lock up and wait in her room next door.

Sliding her notebook from under her pillow, she drew a heavy line through the words 'going into care' and added 'school' beneath 'new shoes' at the bottom of her list. The word school did not fill her with the same dread as going into care had but the thought of starting again in a new class with a new teacher was enough to set her stomach churning.

From on top of the television, the droning buzz of the mobile phone diverted her. Cautiously, she pressed the receiver button and listened. At the other end, a woman's voice, faint and crackly, said hello.

'Hello?' Louisa May replied.

'Is that Miss Frankish?'

'No, it's me.'

There was a short laugh, followed by a loud click as the sound amplified. 'Who's me?' enquired the now-booming voice.

'Louisa May Haddock,' she replied automatically after years of repeating her name fully over housing officers' desktops.

There followed a single, sharp breath. 'Louisa May,' the woman repeated.

'Yes.'

'Oh. So it's Louisa May.' The caller made it seem as if her name was the answer to a hard question with which the teacher had stumped the whole class, but which was so obvious once it had been revealed.

'After Louisa May Alcott,' Louisa May added. There was another 'oh'.

'We don't want any double glazing,' she said, knowing Joanna was always being pestered and presuming from all the pauses this was another canvasser.

'Louisa May, I'm your . . . I'm Wendy Almond. Have you heard about me?'

A shiver crawled up the back of Louisa May's legs, absorbing her whole body slowly and steadily like a hesitant child entering a swimming pool. 'Yes,' Louisa May whispered, 'you're my grandma.'

Sixteen

'Then what did she say?' Joanna demanded, reversing wildly into the main road. Louisa May had begged her to take her to see Georgette straight away. There was so much news, she knew she would die if she had to wait until tea-time. 'Did she tell you how much you were getting? Are diamonds involved?'

'I don't know. We didn't talk about stuff like that,' Louisa May replied evasively. There were some things she didn't want to share with Joanna, things that were for Georgette's ears only. 'The phone went all funny just after she said she was coming to Wathsea.'

'Trust the batteries to run flat on the most important conversation of your life. I only put them in the other day, too. Did she say when she'd be coming?'

Louisa May clung on to her seat belt, partly to protect herself from Joanna's driving, partly to give herself something to stop her hands shaking. Hearing Wendy Almond's voice had both thrilled and terrified her.

'Did she say when?' Joanna prompted, slowing down as traffic built up on Wathsea High Street.

'No, just how.'

'How what?'

'How she knew our address.'

'I gave it to the solicitors,' Joanna began, then frowned. 'No, I didn't. I only gave my number, in case your mum changed her mind about meeting her. How did she know about the hotel?'

'I sent the "between parlours" letter to the library in

Lincoln and it passed my letter to her daughter, who's a librarian in Doncaster.'

'Why?'

'We lived there once,' she replied vaguely. She remembered the first book in the row on the dressing table and smiled.

'So?' Joanna prodded.

'So she, my Auntie Aylsa . . .' Louisa May's tongue fizzed as she named her out loud, 'my Auntie Aylsa sent a fax to all the regional libraries to give all the "between parlours" letters to her and she sent them to my . . . to Wendy Almond. They knew there couldn't be many Haddocks around.'

'I'll resist commenting on that one!' Joanna grinned as she accelerated towards Kesteven.

An auxiliary was scraping the remains of Georgette's minced beef cobbler into his slop tray, talking non-stop, when Louisa May arrived, eager-faced and bursting with news. He scowled at her for interrupting his routine but she was too excited to notice.

'Guess what?' she said, squeezing her mother's arm tightly. 'Mrs Chambers came this morning. It's all right for me to stay with Joanna until you're home. We didn't need to make up that stuff about twins. They hadn't got anyone to foster me anyway!'

Georgette reached out for a hug. 'That's excellent news.' Holding Louisa May close she whispered in her ear. 'Better still, you've saved me from Mr Bailey. If he'd told me one more thing about his verrucas I'd have screamed.'

Louisa May chuckled, staying where she was until the trolley wheels squealed out of earshot.

'Now,' Georgette began, pulling Louisa May upright, 'I want to hear everything.'

As Louisa May repeated her conversation with Wendy Almond, word-for-word, Georgette listened intently, shaking her head in disbelief when the saga of the library books was revealed. 'Tch! Just like Hansel and Gretel with the breadcrumbs,' she said.

There was a short silence until Louisa May commented absent-mindedly, 'I hadn't thought about others.'

'Others?'

She nodded, furrowing her eyebrows in concentration. 'Like Auntie Aylsa. She's Gary's half-sister because Wendy Almond divorced Gary's dad when he was four and married Mr Almond later. So that's why she's an Almond not a Pritchard but Gary kept his name. And then there's . . . ' Louisa May paused, trying to get the names right.

Georgette interrupted. 'It all seems very complicated.' Her voice trembled. 'I hadn't thought about others, either. They're not all going to come are they? It's all too much too soon. I'm scared, Louisa May.'

Louisa May held on to her arm. 'It's all right. Wendy Almond's scared too! She told me. She says she'll wait to hear from you first and to take your time. I told her about who we thought she was. She was upset, then, and said she was sorry if she sounded bossy in the letter, it's just that she hasn't got any grandchildren . . . I've got her number, to call her as soon as you're better. She sounds really nice. She says she can send us a cheque if that will help but she hasn't got much because Mr Almond only gets a disability allowance. He's got funny bowels.'

Georgette was not listening. 'But look at me, Louisa May, what's she going to think when she sees me?'

'Nothing. She just wants to meet us.'

'Can't we just . . . can't we just move on, get back to how we used to be?'

Louisa May shook her head firmly, ignoring the pleading look in her mother's eyes. She had guessed Georgette might want to run away as usual. 'Please, Mum, no. I'm not going through all that again. Joanna made me listen to her about TB last night.'

'I'm nearly better. I'm taking all my tablets.'

'It can come back, just with somebody breathing on you, it can come back—especially if we keep living in damp houses and sharing with other poor people.'

Georgette stared, watery-eyed and resentful, at the plastic bottles of pills. 'And what does Miss Fix-it suggest? A villa in the south of France? We're homeless, remember! And we were homeless before the letters arrived, just like we'll be homeless now they've stopped.'

Undeterred, Louisa May leaned across and whispered in her mother's ear. 'There's five hundred pounds of Gary's insurance left. Wendy says we're welcome to it. His wife let her have half the money, which is only fair because they were getting divorced when he crashed. His wife kept the house.'

'His wife? He had a wife?' This seemed to startle Georgette more than the news of the money.

'He married her after you broke his heart. She was called Kerri,' Louisa May furnished.

'Ugh!'

'I knew you'd say that.'

'It doesn't alter anything. Five hundred pounds won't buy us a house.'

Louisa May bit back her disappointment. The inheritance had seemed a huge amount to her, not quite in Penrose the Pig's league, perhaps, but more than she'd ever known. 'Not even a little one?' she persisted.

'No.'

'A flat?'

'No.'

'A hut?'

Georgette glanced at the telephone directory she had planned to scour after dinner and her expression softened. She touched Louisa May lightly on the arm. 'It's a start, though. We could buy some warm clothes for winter and hire blankets from Lady Putlock.'

The light flooded back into Louisa May's eyes. 'And sit near the window. She couldn't stop us sitting near the window, now, could she? We're "haves".'

Georgette shrugged, pulling the fox-fur out of her bedside cabinet and winding it round her neck. 'I suppose it would be nice to settle somewhere for a while, somewhere I could . . . research my family tree. Cliff Top Villas is as good as anywhere for the moment.' Her voice rose as she stroked the fox-fur over and over with the flat of her hand, as if grooming it for a show. 'I thought I'd begin at the hospital where I was left. One of the nurses here told me they never forget an abandoned baby; it stays with you, especially if you named it. If I can find my nurse, it'll be a start.'

Scraping the bedside chair nearer, Louisa May sat down, dug her elbows into the covers and grinned happily at her mother. Georgette's face glowed with the same fiery determination as the day before. There was also a restlessness about her, her legs shuffling continuously as if impatient to get started.

It was then Louisa May realized just how great the changes to her life were going to be. There would be no back-tracking this time, no running, no pretending. Wendy Almond and Gary Pritchard had seen to all that.

Blood pounded in her ears now, a celebratory drumbeat just for her. They were out of the vicious circle. Not rich, not even safe from homelessness or illness, but out of the circle that had been growing tighter year by year.

A thought struck her. 'I'll be able to have friends to tea, won't I? Like normal kids?'

'Tea?' Georgette asked vaguely. She looked up and smiled at her daughter. 'Ah! Tea! You mean cream tea and seed cake,' she said, putting on her 'Rosanna' voice.

'Cucumber sandwiches and lemonade!' Louisa May added, joining readily in the pretend game.

Georgette stuck her nose in the air like a snooty hostess. 'I wonder if Gilbert would consider an invitation?'

'Or the girl with pink socks so I can throw chicken nuggets at her?'

'What about me?' boomed Joanna's voice from behind them. 'If there's food going, I want in!'

Louisa May grinned and pulled Joanna on to the bed. 'You'll be there anyway, won't she, Mama? We want Auntie Joanna with us.'

Georgette's eyes met Joanna's and a look of understanding passed between them. 'Your Auntie Joanna will always find ginger nuts waiting for her in our parlour.'

'In the parlour, not between?' Joanna teased.

Georgette kissed the fox-fur's nose. 'We are delighted to announce that we are no longer "between parlours".'

122

Seventeen

'They're the ones, aren't they?' Georgette asked, pointing towards the 'Kickstarts'. Louisa May nodded, her eyes darting between the window display and her mother's pale profile, watching anxiously, scared in case she fainted or coughed or turned blue.

Louisa May could not believe they were here, doing something so ordinary as shopping when her mother had only just been discharged from hospital. They had not even been back to the hotel because Georgette insisted on coming to Batty's first. 'New start, new shoes,' she told her firmly in the car.

Joanna had thought it was a great idea, dropping them off with a cheery wave before speeding away, leaving Louisa May feeling lost and deserted, until Georgette had propelled her through the mahogany doors. 'You'll see her later. I'm back now, I'll look after you,' she had said, linking her arm. A mellowness had filled her then, as the words settled inside her like petals falling on moss.

This was how it should be—both of them together again with Joanna as a friendly figure in the background. Always there, like a big sister or a favourite auntie.

Louisa May snatched one last glimpse through the glass of the door. Tonight, she would show Joanna her Worries List, show her how it had all been crossed through, thanks to her. Then she was going to persuade her to call home to Cheadle, if she dared. Now, though, she was here with her mum, buying shoes like before. Only this time it was so different.

The shoe shop was empty, apart from a middle-aged man in a dark suit glowering into the till. He slammed the drawer closed with a hollow 'zing' as they approached. This must be the famous Samuel Batty, Louisa May guessed; Deaky's mean and wicked uncle.

He did not look either; just fed-up. Up close, his untrimmed grey hair flicked along the edge of an over-tight shirt collar. His suit had a worn sheen to it, the kind she often saw dangling from wire coat-hangers in charity shops.

After casting them half a glance, the manager's jaded eyes returned to his inert till. Saturday was the only day Batty's trade was guaranteed; the rest of the week was a write-off. He doubted the odd-looking woman in front of him was going to boost his takings.

The 'odd-looking woman' ran her finger across the wooden counter, then examined her dusty fingertips minutely. 'Mmm. A shame to let such fine furniture deteriorate for want of a little beeswax, don't you agree?'

Mr Batty scowled at the counter, then at Georgette. 'May I help you, madam?' he asked gruffly.

'No, I'm afraid you can't. My custom is reserved for your assistant manager, Mr Deacon, if you don't mind.'

The owner bristled. 'Mr Deacon, my temporary junior, some might say very temporary and very junior, is re-arranging the new insoles at the moment.'

'We'll wait,' Georgette said lightly, strolling to the velvet seats they had taken on their first visit. Pointedly, she brushed the velour covering before sitting down.

'Are you feeling all right? Not hot or anything? When should you have your next tablet?' Louisa May fretted.

Her mother beamed at her through clear, healthy eyes. 'I'm feeling fine. How about you?' she asked.

Louisa May shrugged happily, shuffling on to the seat next to her. 'I'm fine too. You're home and I'm getting new shoes. I'm fine as anything!'

Georgette gazed around, breathing in deeply. 'It's so good to be out in the world again, away from rattling trolleys and nosy doctors.' Unclipping her purse, she took out the cheque Wendy Almond had sent to her in the hospital yesterday, held it up to the light, then shook her head. 'I still can't believe it,' she said.

Louisa May clung protectively to her own inheritance; a padded envelope full of photographs, diaries, and letters. Special letters, unopened and addressed to 'My Baby' which her father had written to her on every birthday.

'Cried me eyes out when I found them,' Wendy had told her. 'That's what started me off on my quest.'

Louisa May thought she might cry her eyes out, too, when she felt strong enough to read them. Meanwhile, Georgette still needed watching. 'Put it away, Mum. I don't want you lending it out to you-know-who,' she whispered urgently.

Georgette glanced at the cheque again then folded it back into her purse. 'Once, Louisa May, once I lent him some money. I'm hardly likely to repeat my mistake, am I?'

'I don't know. You might.'

'Of course I won't. I have other business to attend to here,' she said mysteriously. 'Ah! We are about to be served.'

Stephen Deacon came towards them, fixing his 'friendly and helpful assistant' smile across his face, which turned into a 'surprised and unsure assistant' smirk as he realized who his customers were.

It had been over a week since Louisa May had seen him, then it had been from a distance as he scurried to his room. Every evening, Wanda eyed his empty table with mascaraed yearning, brushing aside Ambrose's dark hints about back-rent and 'one-rule-for-one-and-not-the-other'. Joanna reckoned Sneaky Deaky was as 'skint as a skunk'.

The debtor flashed his smile. 'Georgette! You look so well. How are you?' he gushed. He really did seem pleased to see her, Louisa May thought. Georgette's face flamed a heroine-pink like the women on her book covers and Louisa May began to wonder if Georgette's 'business' had anything to do with buying shoes at all.

She sat patiently, swinging her feet beneath the chair as Georgette described the treatment she had undergone in hospital, using her 'Rosanna' voice more and more as Stephen's interest grew.

'I couldn't believe it when I heard. TB!' he trilled.

'I suspected the worst during our evening together.'

'You should have said.'

'It doesn't matter.'

'It's been so dull at the hotel without you.'

'I can imagine, but we shall be staying on for a while—until the end of the season, at least, should you care for a stroll.'

Louisa May tuned contentedly in and out of the conversation. Other parents did this, chatting on and on in shops and supermarkets while their kids hung about, bored. It was normal. No hiding behind books today. No making her do the talking to the grown-ups. Georgette was being normal, just like she had always wanted her to be. Eventually, she decided she would be normal, too. 'Mum. The Kickstarts? Like, this year?' she whined, imitating the girl with pink socks.

Georgette laughed. 'Yes, of course. Louisa May needs some new shoes, please, Stephen. Kickstarts. The ones in patent leather with the multi-coloured laces. I hope you've got her size, after all this.'

The assistant glanced at Louisa May's feet. 'You certainly know how to get the most out of a pair of shoes, young lady.'

'I've had to,' Louisa May retorted. 'Not having anyone to lend me the price of new ones.' She shrugged off each shoe and grinned at her socks. They were baggy and dirty and dishwater grey. They probably stank. She hoped they did. Hoped they stank worse than a dead dog. 'I think I'm a three,' she said, aiming her left foot to within an inch of his nose. He grimaced and leaned back. Her grin deepened. That would teach him to ignore people when they needed help.

'Do you fancy Stephen Deacon?' Louisa May asked as they began their walk up the steep hill.

Her mother arched her eyebrows. 'I don't,' she eventually replied, 'but Rosanna does.'

Louisa May bent down again to wipe a smudge of dirt from her Kickstarts. 'Well, she wants to make sure he's kind and reliable. The sort that wouldn't let her down in an emergency.'

'She will. She's not daft.'

'That's all right, then.'

Further up the hill, mother and daughter gazed out at the sea. Louisa May's heart soared, as it always did, as she searched the horizon for ships bound for home. 'He was a nice man, that Daniel Brody,' she said.

Georgette clung to her protectively. 'Yes, he was.'

'Not much of a writer, though.'

'Not much of an anything, really, but he got us through some hard times.'

'Would Gary Pritchard have got us through?'

'I don't know. I doubt it, to be honest.' Georgette glanced at Louisa May's parcel. 'He must have thought more of you than I realized,' she admitted. 'I'm sorry.'

'It's a shame he's dead. Motor-bike accident.'

The glittering waves broke silently on the beach beneath them, leaving foamy smiles on the damp sand. 'You'll be able to find out more about him when Wendy Almond comes,' Georgette said quietly.

Louisa May held her breath. 'When will that be?' she asked.

'Soon,' Georgette promised. 'Soon.'

Leaning her head against her mother's shoulder, Louisa May swallowed, her throat aching with unasked questions. Soon. Soon she would meet her grandma, start school, move home. Soon everything would be all right. For her. She hesitated. 'What if your mum's dead when you find her?'

Georgette shrugged away the suggestion. 'Oh, she's not dead. I'd have known. I'd have felt it.'

'Blimey! I'll have more grandmas than I know what to do with. Christmas will be good this year!'

Laughing, Georgette rubbed her arms with the cold. 'I wish I hadn't left my fur in Joanna's car,' she said through chattering teeth.

Immediately, Louisa May began to panic. 'Let's get back to the hotel, quick. You must need a tablet by now. And Dr Beecham said you had to eat plenty of fruit and vegetables. There's some grapes in our room and the bed's made and we've hired an extra blanket because Wanda's turned the heating back down—'

Her outburst was cut short by Georgette covering her ears with her hands. 'Stop fussing, Louisa May! Who's the mother here?'

'You are.'

'Right then, let's go.' With her arm round Louisa May she guided her only child across the road and towards the hotel, teasing her all the way. 'Just look at your hair! When was the last time you brushed it? And fasten your coat—you'll catch your death! Mind you don't scrape your new shoes; money doesn't grow on trees, you know! And if you're starting school you should be learning your tables. What's six sevens? Five eights?'

Louisa May begged her to stop. 'I think I preferred Mrs Van Der Lees!' she complained.

Instantly, Georgette's theatrical eyebrow arched like a cat's back. 'That can be arranged, my dear!' As she elbowed open the hotel door she sniffed and turned to Louisa May. 'Ah! Mildew, mould, and madness. How heavenly! Shall we?' she asked.

'We shall, Mama. Perkins is expecting us.'

'You mean he's watered down the ketchup?'

'Exactly!'

'Splendid!'

Arm-in-arm, Georgette and Louisa May swanned grandly into the hotel, oblivious to the darkness which engulfed them.

Other Oxford children's novels

Dragon's Rock   Tim Bowler
ISBN 0 19 271693 X

For Benjamin sleep had become a place of fear, where the dragon with its roaring fury hunted him. But now he had the chance to go back to Dragon's Rock and put things right. And then maybe the dragon would leave him alone.

River Boy   Tim Bowler
ISBN 0 19 271756 1

It didn't start with the river boy. It started as so many things started, with Grandpa, and with swimming. It was only later, when she came to think things over, that she realized that in a strange way the river boy had been part of her all along, like the figment of a dream. And the dream was her life.

It's My Life   Michael Harrison
ISBN 0 19 271749 9

Martin knew something was wrong as soon as he stepped into the hall. He should have turned round and walked straight out again. But he didn't and within minutes he finds himself in the middle of a nightmare. He is kidnapped and held captive on a canal boat—but that is only the beginning. When Martin finds out who his kidnapper is, and who he is in league with, the horror deepens and Martin has to use all his ingenuity to escape—with Hannah's help.

Firebug   Susan Gates
ISBN 0 19 271735 9

When Callum sets fire to his own home to take revenge on his
mother's boyfriend, Nick, he has no idea of the disastrous chain of
events he will set in motion. Who is the weird android-like figure
crouching by the incubator at the chemical company where his dad
works? Why is Dad having secret meetings with Nick? And what is
happening to the trees in the forest? Throughout all these strange
events, the squirrel seems to be the only thing Callum can rely on.

Iron Heads   Susan Gates
ISBN 0 19 271755 3

When Rachel's parents get jobs on an off-shore island, her main
worry is when the wind turbine will be installed so that she can play
her CDs. But then she notices some weird things happening. Her
brother, Stevie, always untidy, insists that everything in his room
should be in straight lines facing the same way. Why do the island
rabbits dig their burrows in parallel lines, facing north? Why don't
the islanders get lost in the fog? And why did the last warden's house
burn down?

As she tries to find the answers to these mysteries, Rachel has to
act quickly to prevent another tragedy.

The Lost Mine   Pamela Grant
ISBN 0 19 271659 X

Jamie has always known that he cannot go underground into the
mines. It is his worst nightmare; the secret fear that has haunted him
all his life. But he also knows that when he is fourteen, without fail,
the Company will send him deep down into the earth. There is
nothing else for Jamie to do in this mining village, and if he doesn't
work his family won't eat.

Cuckoos   Roger J. Green
ISBN 0 19 271792 8

John's threats were like a cuckoo's egg. Once laid, they stayed there and pushed everything else out of your life.

Sam Wilkinson has become the latest target of John Snow's bullying tactics. Even though there is no physical violence, John's threats and insults have the power to bring Sam's world crashing down around him. And when nobody will listen, Sam decides the time has come for him to take action. But Sam's attempt to stand up for himself has consequences that could not have been foreseen, especially by John . . .

Witchy   Ann Phillips
ISBN 0 19 271794 4

Thrown out of home on suspicion of being a witch, twelve-year-old Aggie has to make her own way in the harsh world of the Fens in the 1890s. But wherever she goes, the gossip follows her, until she almost comes to believe it herself. 'If I got seeing and knowing,' she asks her gran, 'am I a witch?'

Aggie hopes she can put the past behind her and make a new life for herself; but then comes news from home and Aggie is thrust back into a life of superstition and hate.

The Bowman of Crécy   Ronald Welch
ISBN 0 19 271746 4

Set in the fourteenth century, the story follows the adventures of Hugh Fletcher and his loyal band of outlaws who live in the forests on the English-Welsh border. Hugh is offered a commission in Sir John Carey's company to take part in King Edward III's campaign against France, culminating in the battle of Crécy, an experience which changes the whole course of Hugh's life.

Oxford Children's Modern Classics

The Ship That Flew   Hilda Lewis
ISBN 0 19 271768 5

Peter sees the model ship in the shop window and he wants it more than anything else on earth. But it is no ordinary model. The ship takes Peter and his brother and sisters on magical flights, wherever they ask to go. They fly around the world and back into the past. But how long can you keep a ship that is worth everything in the world, and a bit over . . . ?

A Little Lower than the Angels   Geraldine McCaughrean
ISBN 0 19 271780 4
Winner of the Whitbread Children's Novel Award

Gabriel has no idea what the future will hold when he runs away from his apprenticeship with the bad-tempered stonemason. But God Himself, in the shape of playmaster Garvey, has plans for him. He wants Gabriel for his angel . . .

But will Gabriel's new life with the travelling players be any more secure? In a world of illusion, people are not always what they seem. Least of all Gabriel.

Minnow on the Say   Philippa Pearce
ISBN 0 19 271778 2

David couldn't believe his eyes. Wedged by the landing stage at the bottom of the garden was a canoe. The *Minnow*. David traces the canoe's owner, Adam, and they begin a summer of adventures. The *Minnow* takes them on a treasure hunt along the river. But they are not the only people looking for the treasure, and soon they are caught in a race against time . . .

Tom's Midnight Garden   Philippa Pearce
ISBN 0 19 271793 6 (hardback)   0 19 271777 4 (paperback)
Winner of the Carnegie Medal

Tom has to spend the summer at his aunt's and it seems as if
nothing good will ever happen again. Then he hears the grandfather
clock strike thirteen—and everything changes. Outside the door is a
garden—a garden that shouldn't exist. Are the children there
ghosts—or is it Tom who is the ghost?

The Eagle of the Ninth   Rosemary Sutcliff
ISBN 0 19 271765 0

The Ninth Legion marched into the mists of northern Britain. And
they never came back. Four thousand men disappeared and the Eagle
standard was lost.

Marcus Aquila, a young Roman officer, has to find out what
happened to his father and the Ninth Legion. He embarks on a quest
into the unknown territory of the north. A quest so hazardous that
no one expects him to return . . .

Outcast   Rosemary Sutcliff
ISBN 0 19 271766 9

Sickness and death come to the tribe. They said it was because of
Beric, because he had brought down the Anger of the Gods. The
warriors of the tribe cast him out. Alone without friends, family or
tribe, Beric faced the dangers of the Roman World.

The Silver Branch   Rosemary Sutcliff
ISBN 0 19 271764 2

Violence and intrigue are undermining Rome's influence in Britain.
And in the middle of the unrest, Justin and Flavius uncover a plot to
overthrow the Emperor. In fear for their lives, they find themselves
leading a tattered band of loyalists into the thick of battle in defence
of the honour of Rome.

The Lantern Bearers   Rosemary Sutcliff

ISBN 0 19 271763 4
Winner of the Carnegie Medal

The last of the Roman army have set sail and left Britain for ever. They have abandoned the country to civil war and the threat of Saxon invasion. When his home and all he loves are destroyed, Aquila endures years of torment. He fights to bring some meaning back into his life, and with it the hope of revenge . . .

Brother in the Land   Robert Swindells

ISBN 0 19 271785 5

Danny's life will never be the same again. He is one of the unlucky ones. A survivor. One of those who have come through a nuclear holocaust alive. He records the sights and events around him, all the time struggling to keep himself and his brother alive.